"STIRRING . . .
COMPELLING . . .
EXTRAORDINARY . . .

Perceptively reveals the elaborate emotional lives of several people: Hy Dodd and her older sister, Glady Jo Cleary, best friends; Anna Neale, the group's 73-year-old founder, once Glady Joe's housekeeper; Anna's spirited only daughter, Marianna; Sophia Darling, a superb swimmer who has drowned herself in marriage and three kids; Em Reed, joined to a philanderer; Hy's friend Corinna Amurri, done in by wars; and Constance, who consorts with Em's husband when her own dies unexpectedly. . . .Their lives are the squares, their words the designs, their gestures the stitches that hold this book together as surely as an extraordinary quilt."

—*Detroit Free Press*

"The tales are of love and betrayal, dreams and losses. . . . In quilting, Whitney Otto finds an illuminating framework within which to view women's lives. . . . She excellently uses her central metaphor, taking us from discussion of quilting in wartime to the story of a woman's son killed in Vietnam, from preserving quilts to preserving marriages, from the patterns of quilts to the patterns of women's lives."

—*The Cleveland Plain Dealer*

Please turn the page for more critical acclaim. . . .

"A RADIANT WORK
OF ART . . .

It is about mothers and daughters; it is about the estrangement and intimacy between generations. It is a compelling tale that is history-haunted and ridden with secrets. . . . Like the sashing that binds together the blocks of a quilt, Otto alternates these chapters with sets of quilting 'instructions.' These combine quilting technique and lore with lessons in American history and musings of the heart."
—The Seattle Times

"Moving . . . The structure of the story is deceptively simple: Finn Bennett-Dodd, granddaughter of one of the quilters, comes to stay with her great-aunt Glady Joe and grandmother Hy while she considers her impending marriage. The stories she hears—and the things not said—become a compelling lesson on women's changing roles and expectations."
—Los Angeles Daily News

"Engaging . . . Ms. Otto has written an affecting book about how an American quilt is made out of the tales of terror and delight pieced together by eight diverse, yet profoundly related, American women."
—Dallas Morning News

By Whitney Otto
Published by Ballantine Books:

HOW TO MAKE AN AMERICAN QUILT
NOW YOU SEE HER

Books published by The Ballantine Publishing
Group are available at quantity discounts on bulk
purchases for premium, educational, fund-raising,
and special sales use. For details, please call
1-800-733-3000.

HOW TO MAKE AN AMERICAN QUILT

Whitney Otto

BALLANTINE BOOKS • NEW YORK

Grateful acknowledgment is made to the following for permission to reprint previously published material: NEW DIRECTIONS PUBLISHING CORP.: Excerpt from "In You: The Earth" from *The Captain's Verses* by Pablo Neruda. Copyright © 1972 by Pablo Neruda and Donald D. Walsh. VIKING PENGUIN: Excerpt from "The Veteran" from *The Portable Dorothy Parker* by Dorothy Parker. Copyright 1926, renewed 1954 by Dorothy Parker. Reprinted by permission of the publisher, Viking Penguin, a division of Penguin Books USA, Inc. WARNER/CHAPPELL MUSIC, INC.: Excerpt from "You'd Be So Nice to Come Home To" by Cole Porter. Copyright © 1979 by Chappell & Co. All rights reserved. Used by permission.

Author photo: John Riley

Detail of quilt courtesy of The Metropolitan Museum of Art, Sansbury-Mills Fund, 1974. (1974.24)

Library of Congress Catalog Card Number: 90-48233

ISBN 0-345-37080-5

This edition published by arrangement with Villard Books, a division of Random House, Inc.

Manufactured in the United States of America

First Ballantine Books Edition: April 1992

20 19 18 17 16 15 14 13

For John

[On photography:] "One theme with endless variations, like life itself."

ALFRED STEIGLITZ

When I was young and bold and strong,
Oh, right was right, and wrong was wrong!
My plume on high, my flag unfurled,
I rode away to right the world.
"Come out, you dogs, and fight!" said I,
And wept there was but once to die.

But I am old; and good and bad
Are woven in a crazy plaid.

DOROTHY PARKER

Contents

A Note from the Author

In researching my novel, I found the following books particularly helpful in providing quilting details: *Twentieth Century Quilts, 1900–1950* by Thomas K. Woodward and Blanche Greenstein (New York: E. P. Dutton, 1988), and *Hearts & Hands* by Pat Ferrero, Elaine Hedges, and Julie Silber (San Francisco: Quilt Digest Press, 1987). The work of Setsuko Segawa is a wonderful example of the quilt as fine art; she has a number of books out on the subject as well.

I cannot thank these authors enough and I strongly recommend their books to anyone interested in quilting.

I also wish to thank the PBS series *Eyes on the Prize: 1954–1965*.

Prologue

AT FIRST, I THOUGHT I WOULD STUDY ART. ART HIS-
tory, to be exact. Then I thought, No, what about
physical anthropology?—a point in my life thereaf-
ter referred to as My Jane Goodall Period. I tried to
imagine my mother, Sarah Bennett-Dodd (called
Sally by everyone with the exception of her
mother), camping with me in the African bush,
drinking strong coffee from our battered tin cups,
much in the way that Jane did with Mrs. Goodall. I saw us laid up with matching cases of malaria;
in mother/daughter safari shorts; our hands weath-
ering in exactly the same fashion.

Then, of course, I remembered that I was talking
about *my* mother, Sally, who is most comfortable
with modernity and refuses to live in a house that
anyone has lived in before, exposing me to a life of
tract housing that was curious and awful.

Literature was my next love. Until I became
loosely acquainted with critical theory, which
struck me as a kind of intellectualism for its own
sake. It always seems that one has to choose literature or critical theory, that one cannot love both.

1

All of this finally pushed me willingly (I later realized) into history.

I began with the discipline of the time line—a holdover from elementary school—setting all the dates in order, allowing me to fix time and place. History needs a specific context, if nothing else. My time lines gradually grew more and more ornate, with pasted-on photographs and drawings that I carefully cut from cheap history books possessing great illustrations but terrible, unchallenging text. I was taken with the *look* of history before I arrived at the "meat" of the matter. But the construction of the time line is both horizontal and vertical, both distance and depth. Which, finally, makes it rather unwieldy on paper. What I am saying is that it needed other dimensions, that history is not a matter of dates, and only disreputable or unimaginative teachers take the "impartial" date approach, thereby killing all interest in the subject at a very early age for many students.

(I knew, in a perfect world, I would not be forced to choose a single course of study, that I would have time for all these interests. I could gather up all my desires and count them out like valentines.)

The Victorians caught my eye almost instantly with their strange and sometimes ugly ideas about architecture and dress and social conventions. Some of it was pure whimsy, like a diorama in which ninety-two squirrels were stuffed and mounted, enacting a basement beer-and-poker party, complete with cigars and green visors pulled low over their bright eyes; or a house that displayed a painting of cherubs, clad in strips of white linen, flying above the clouds with an identical painting hidden, right next to it, under a curtain in which the same cherubs—babies though they were—are completely nude. Or a privileged Texas belle's curio cabinet that contained a human skull and blackened hand. Or still another young woman (wealthy daughter of a prominent man) who insisted on gliding through the family mansion with a handful of live kittens clinging to the train of her dress.

I enrolled in graduate school. Then I lost interest. I cared and then I didn't care. I wanted to know as much about the small, odd details that I discovered here and there when looking into the past as I did about Lenin's secret train or England's Victorian imperialism or a flawless neo-Marxist critique of capitalism.

There were things that struck me as funny, like the name Bushrod Washington, which belonged to George's nephew, or the man who painted Mary Freake and her baby, known only as the Freake Limner. And I like that sort of historical gossip; I mean, is it true that Catherine the Great died trying to copulate with a horse? And if not, what a strange thing to say about someone. Did Thomas Jefferson have a lengthy, fruitful affair with his slave Sally Hemings? What does that say about the man who was the architect of the great democratic dream? What does it say about us? Did we inherit the dream or the illicit, unsettling racial relationship?

This sort of thing is not considered scholarly or academic or of consequence, these small footnotes. And perhaps rightly so. Of course, I loved the important, rigorous historical inquiry as well. What I think I wanted was both things, the silly and the sublime; which adds up to a whole picture, a grudgingly true past. And out of that past truth a present reality.

You could say I was having trouble linking the two.

I wished for history to be vital, alive with the occasional quirk of human nature (a little "seriojovial"); I imagined someone saying to me, *Finn, what ever gave you the idea that history was any sort of living thing? Really. Isn't that expectation just the least bit contradictory?*

Then Sam asked me to marry him.

It seemed to me a good idea.

Yet it somehow led me back to my educational concern, which was how to mesh halves into a whole, only in this case it was how to make a successful link of unmarried to married, man to woman, the merging of the roads before us. When Heathcliff ran away from Wuthering Heights, he left Cathy wild and sad, howling on the moors, *I am Heathcliff*, as if their love were so powerful, their souls so seamlessly mated, that no division existed for them, save the corporeal (though I tend to believe they got "together" at least once), which is of little consequence in the presence of the spirit.

All of which leaves me wondering, astonished, and a little put off. How does one accomplish such a fusion of selves? And, if the affection is that strong, how does one *avoid* it, leaving a little room for the person you once were? The balance of marriage, the delicate, gentle shifting of the polished scales.

Let me say that I like Sam tremendously. I love him truly.

The other good idea was spending the summer with my grandmother Hy Dodd and her sister Glady Joe Cleary. Their relationship with me is different from that with the other grandchildren; we share secrets. And I probably talk to them a little more than my cousins or their own children do. I think they have a lot to say and I am more than willing to hear it. All of it. Whatever strikes them as important.

To me, they are important.

So my days are now spent watching the quilters come and go, lazily eavesdropping on the hum of their conversation and drifting off into dreams on my great-aunt's generous porch; thinking about my Sam, my sweetheart. Or lying on my back, in the shade, in Aunt Glady's extravagant garden, removing the ice cubes from my tea, running them across my face, neck, and chest in an effort to cool down from the heat.

I could wander over to the Grasse swimming pool, but it is always so crowded. Sophia Richards says you never know who you'll meet there—as if I want to meet anyone. As if I am not already staying in a house that has quite a bit of "foot traffic."

The quilters have offered to make a bridal quilt in honor of my marriage, but I tell them to *Please continue with what you are doing as if I never arrived to stay for the summer.* Sometimes I say, *I can't think about that now* (as if anyone can think clearly in this peppery heat). I can see this puzzles them, makes them wonder what sort of girl it is who "cannot think about" her own wedding.

This amuses me as well, since, at age twenty-six, I have lost track of the sort of girl that I am. I used to be a young scholar; I am now an engaged woman. Not that you cannot be both—even I understand that—yet I cannot fathom who I think I am *at this time*. My aunt Glady told me recently that this strikes her as "healthy and sensible"—to take a minute or so for yourself, to take a little time to think.

The true source of my interest during this visit, this impasse in my own life, is Anna Neale, another one of the quilters and my aunt's oldest friend. Anna has promised me a long talk one day, she says, when she is not so busy, when there is nothing else to do. But her time always seems occupied. She's remarkably beautiful, Anna Neale is. Even at seventy-three. She can turn heads.

We are all drawn to beauty. I think it is a beacon for us; makes us want to listen.

Well, I am ready to listen.

Instructions No. 1

WHAT YOU NEED:
You need a large wooden frame and enough space to accommodate it. Put comfortable chairs around it, allowing for eight women of varying ages, weight, coloring, and cultural orientation. It is preferable that this large wood frame be located in a room in a house in Atwater or Los Banos or a small town outside Bakersfield called Grasse. It should be a place that gets a thick, moist blanket of tule fog in the winter and be hot as blazes in the summer. Fix plenty of lemonade. Cookies are a nice complement.

When you choose your colors, make them sympathetic to one another. Consider the color wheel of grammar school—primary colors, phenomena of light and dark; avoid antagonism of hues—it detracts from the pleasure of the work. Think of music as you orchestrate the shades and patterns; pretend that you are a conductor in a lush symphony hall, imagine the audience saying *Ooh* and *Ahh* as they applaud your work.

Patterns with tiny, precise designs always denote twentieth-century taste.

Your needles must be finely honed so you do not break the weave of your fabric. The ones from England are preferable. And plenty of good-quality thread, both to bind the pieces and adorn the quilt. Embroidery thread is required for the latter. You will need this to hold the work together for future generations. Unless you are interested in selling your quilt at an art fair or gallery, in which case the quilt will still need to be held together for generations of people you will never meet.

The women who circle the frame should be compatible. Their names are: Sophia, Glady Joe, Hy, Constance, Em, Corrina, Anna, and Marianna. Hyacinth and Gladiola Josephine are sisters, two years apart, and always called Hy and Glady Joe. Anna and Marianna are mother and daughter, seventeen years apart. Em, Sophia, and Corrina are all natives to Grasse, while Constance is a relative newcomer. When you have assembled the group, once a week for better than thirty-five years, give or take some latecomers, you will be ready to begin the traditional, free-form *Crazy Quilt*.

The *Crazy Quilt* was a fad of the nineteenth century and as such is not truly considered Art, yet still it has its devotees. It is comprised of remnants of material in numerous textures, colors; actually, you could not call the squares of a *Crazy Quilt* squares, since the stitched-together pieces are of all sizes and shapes. This is the pattern with the least amount of discipline and the greatest measure of emotion. Considering the eight quilters surrounding the frame in the room of the house in the small town outside Bakersfield called Grasse, considering the more than thirty-five years it will reveal, perhaps some emerging images will be lambs or yellow roses or mermaids, entwined wedding rings or hearts in states of disrepair. You will find this work to be most revealing, not only in the material contributions to the quilt, but in who enjoys sewing them and who does not. This random piecing together.

More Instructions

What you should understand when undertaking the construction of a quilt is that it is comprised of spare time as well as excess material. Something left over from a homemade dress or a man's shirt or curtains for the kitchen window. It utilizes that which would normally be thrown out, "waste," and eliminates the extra, the scraps. And out of that which is left comes a new, useful object.

Take material from clothing that belongs to some family member or friend or lover (if you find yourself to be that sort of a girl). Bind them together carefully. Wonder at the disparity of your life. Finger the patches representing "lover" and meditate on the meaning of illicit love in early American society. Failing that, consider the meaning of the affair in today's time frame.

The Roanoke Island Company, founded by Sir Walter Raleigh in 1585, completely disappeared—all 117 men, women, and children—by 1590 with no one knowing exactly what took place during that five-year period, and a single word carved into a tree the only viable clue: CROATOAN. No historian has figured out what that means. This you will find as the genesis and recurring theme in America as founded by the English: that we are a people fraught with mysteries and clues; there are things that cannot be fathomed.

Do not forget that the Norse, Spanish, French, Italians, and god knows who else arrived before the English, relative latecomers to this place, and that the Indians stood on the shores, awaiting them all. These same Indians were exploited by the English, who were lazy and preferred to spend their time smoking tobacco on the banks of the James River rather than till the soil, expecting "someone else" to do it for them. Killing themselves by the end of the first winter because, as they emphatically told the Indians, *We are not farmers. We are explorers,* then demanded their provisions. Some say this is where the seeds of slavery were sown. An institution the English were not devious enough to come up with on their own, instead adopting it from the Spanish, who had been dealing in African flesh for a number of years. But that is another story.

Consider that women came across the Atlantic from the beginning and were not allowed to vote until 1920. A quick calculation leaves you wondering about those hundreds of years in between. You are curious about their power, their spheres of influence. Most historians agree that the first president voted in by the women was a washout, a different sort of man than Washington, Lincoln, Jefferson, and so on. Men can take credit for those presidents.

Recall that women who came to newly colonized America often outlived their husbands and that it was not uncommon, in those early Virginia days, for them to be widowed and inherit, remarry, be widowed and inherit, remarry, and so on. This, you would think, may have been a frightening cycle to a number of men in the area, never knowing when their number was up, so to speak. But with so few careers open to women at the time, they simply made the best with what they had to work with. Not unlike fashioning a quilt from scraps, if you think about it. And there weren't that many of them, proportionally speaking. With that sort of social arrangement, you find yourself wondering if all these husband deaths were strictly due to natural causes; but to conjecture such a thought, without historical verification, would be to assume the worst about the early settlers. No reputable historian would suggest such a thing: duplicitous, untrustworthy, murderous women. Not just any women, but *wives.*

She used whatever material she had at hand and if she was too overburdened with work she could ask her husband, sweetly, with sugar in her voice, to please, please look into acquiring an indentured servant. England, experiencing a bit of an economic crisis, had a surplus of unemployed citizens it was not much interested in caring for, and Virginia, Tidewater, and Maryland took on the look of an acceptable repository. Ah, but that is to confuse convicts with indentures and, really, they are not the same. An indentured servant is more like a slave, whereas a convict is more like a caged man. Different. You see.

Later, a turn in England's financial fortunes led to

a drop-off of people interested in coming to America as servants, what with renewed opportunity at home (and that unholy Atlantic crossing), and an attempt to fill the resulting American employment gap paved the way for African-American slavery. But that is another story.

The nineteenth century brought an explosion of ideas to the concept of the quilt, of a woman's political voice. Not to mention the domestic conflicts of the Revolutionary War, followed by the Civil War (with one or two small—by comparison—skirmishes in between). Ignore the fact that the Revolution still left some unequal and the Civil War had a rather specific definition of brother against brother, neglecting to include color or gender. That, too, is another story.

Your concern might be trying to reduce your chosen quilt topic to more manageable dimensions. For example, the Revolutionary War could be defined as a bloody betrayal. One can almost hear the voice of Mother England crying, "But you are mine. An extension of me. You promised to be faithful, to send back your riches and keep me in a style to which I have become accustomed." America's answer something like: "I need my space. It isn't that I am not fond of you. We can still maintain a friendly trading relationship."

There is the Civil War, which is a conflict of the blood tie. No one fights dirtier or more brutally than blood; only family knows its own weakness, the exact placement of the heart. The tragedy is that one can still love with the force of hatred. Feel infuriated that once you are born to another, that kinship lasts through life and death, immutable, unchanging, no matter how great the misdeed or betrayal. Blood cannot be denied, and perhaps that is why we fight tooth and claw, because we cannot, being only human, put asunder what God has joined together.

Women were witness to Abraham Lincoln's assassination. Find some quality silk and cotton in red, white, and blue. Cut white stars in the evening as you sit on your summer porch. Appliqué the letters that spell out your name, your country, your grief. Stitch across the quilt a flag held in the beak of a dove. Ponder the fact that you could not vote for the man but will defy any male citizen who will not allow you your measure of sorrow at the president's sudden death. Say something in cloth about the Union lasting, preserved. Listen to the men expound their personal satisfaction in glory of the vote. Listen to them express surprise that you, too, would like to vote and be heard. They might say, *This is not your concern,* and conclude that perhaps you are too idle at home and should consider having another child.

Save your opinions for your quilt. Put your heart and voice into it. Cast your ballot; express your feelings regarding industrialization, emancipation, women's suffrage, your love of family.

Send away for silk ribbon printed with black-lined photolithographs. Try your hand at doing these ink drawings yourself. Experiment with the colors newly available from nineteenth-century factories: peacock blue, scarlet, jade green, eggplant, and amber. Save a scrap of velvet. For texture.

As the nineteenth century draws to a close, be sure to express your gratitude for the "improvements" in your life; you can drive your own buggy, attend college, or work in a textile factory in Lowell, Massachusetts. And do not forget the popular magazines like *Peterson's* or *Godey's Lady's Book*, which encourage the decorative quilt over the story quilt (the quilt with a voice), as it can safely be displayed outside the bedroom without offense. Place it in the parlor. Simply to work a pattern and color with no ulterior thought is the mark of a woman of leisure and reflects well on her husband.

You want to keep these things in mind: history and family. How they are often inseparable. In the twentieth century you may feel that all those things that went before have little to do with you, that you are made immune to the past by the present day: All those dead people and conflicts and ideas—why, they are only stories we tell one another. History and politics and conflict and rebellion and family and betrayal.

Think about it.

The Flower Girls

MANY OF THEIR NEIGHBORS CANNOT RECALL A TIME when Glady Joe and Hy were not "old." It seemed that the two sisters had always been languishing somewhere in their senior years, as if they had somehow executed the leap from girlhood to middle age to senior citizen, lacking any sort of transitional areas in between.

And it seemed that one was seldom seen without the other. Except for that brief time following the death of Hy's husband, James Dodd, but that was a short period and soon all appeared to be back as it was. Even married, the two sisters never lived far apart.

These days they share the house where the quilting circle meets, where Glady Joe had lived with her husband, Arthur Cleary, also deceased. When Arthur was alive, before Hy moved in, the house held their twins, Francie and Kayo, as well as Anna Neale, their housekeeper, and her daughter, Marianna. Anna said, "This is a strange house; haunted, I think it could be said. But it is an odd haunting, not as if something extra were here as much as

15

something missing; not a void, only the powerful absence of a thing lost."

Glady Joe Cleary and Hy Dodd travel each summer in an enormous Chevy station wagon, visiting their children and grandchildren flung like stars across the United States. Hy takes photographs of the places they pass through and the relatives they see. A traveler, taking his own summer vacation, could look up from his roadside lunch or his video camera (weary from recording memories of his vacation with the wife and kids), or simply finish pumping gas somewhere outside Four Corners, shaking his head at the puzzle of anyone *choosing* to live in this hot desert; he would see two elderly women, both with silver hair, faded blue eyes, and soft, lined faces. He would notice the inevitable signs of old age—the hollowing of the cheeks, the loose flesh along the jawline, the tortoiseshell glasses that make the blue eyes appear slightly larger than they truly are. He might admire Hy's sunset-hued blouse and the Mexican lace of her skirt, as she sits facing Glady Joe. Glady Joe sits with her legs crossed, scribbling away in a spiral notebook, now and then looking at her pen accusingly, giving it one or two sharp jerks in an attempt to get the ink flowing again. He might like the smart look of Glady Joe's white cotton men's shirt and white skirt. Or the way Hy's dangling onyx earrings move with the motion of her head.

Another tired tourist could look through the lens of his camera to see Hy directing Glady Joe into a pose, somewhere in the expanse of the green Virginia countryside. He might take a moment of his attention away from *his* tired wife (who is trying to placate their bored, cranky children with promises of ice cream after dinner) to notice an elderly woman, all in white, behaving as irritably as his youngsters, while the other woman, the one with dangling onyx earrings, places her hands on her hips as she lowers the hand holding the camera, her lips drawn into a thin, angry line.

And maybe a woman traveling with her grown daughter would see these same elderly women at a gas station just outside Colorado Springs, sharing soda from a bottle, planning their next stop. And marvel at how alike these women look—except that one is dressed a little more colorfully, more stylishly—so physically alike they must be related. As if their choice in clothing were the only distinguishing feature between them.

When Glady Joe passes by any of these fellow travelers, she leaves an essence of floral scent in her wake, while Hy's perfume is musky, oddly sexual for someone so clearly in her seventies. Hy, too, walks a little less briskly than Glady Joe, more deliberately. Just taking her time. Both women have some of the awkwardness of age in their step, as if moving with a certain amount of care.

Sometimes they pull over to a rest stop and have a smoke. Sharing the cigarette as they shared the soda pop. Once a day, sometimes twice.

The sisters compile a notebook of their favorite restaurants, coffee shops, and roadside snack bars located on the numbered highways they travel. Glady

Joe collects scraps of fabric and lace along the way, checking the remnant bins of fabric stores. She touches the cloth as her mind works its possibilities, her eyes large behind her glasses and far away. She likes to re-create various landmarks and landscapes, her favorite being Virginia with its lush green valleys *(Oh Shenandoah/I love your daughter/I'm bound away/You rolling river)*, farmlands—"God's patchwork," she says—blooming dogwood in pink and white. Hy has a marked preference for historical figures as well as the common man. She is encouraging Glady Joe to agree to do Monticello but Glady Joe will only agree if they leave out the remaining slave quarters in the design.

The west-side view of Jefferson's home is called the Sea View because the extensive grasslands and rolling slopes resemble the ocean.

Hy would prefer to quilt a Native American surrounded by pueblos and mesas, but Glady Joe says that would be as bad as showing Jefferson's slave cabins.

(There are only two ways to deal with tragedy and injustice: show it plainly or hide all traces; and the sisters are in disagreement on this matter.)

"I disagree," says Hy. "I want to show the nobility in the Indian."

"The only thing noble," says Glady Joe, "is how those people managed to survive the theft of their sacred land and the poverty to which they have been reduced."

"You're breaking my heart," says Hy.

Which makes Glady Joe furious. "Your heart

should be more than broken, it should be shattered."

"What about government reparation?" asks Hy.

"What about it?" retorts Glady Joe.

"We could call the quilt 'God's People,' " says Hy after a brief pause.

Glady Joe grips the wheel of the Chevy. "You mean 'God's Forgotten People.' " Glady Joe's fury is directed at her sister, but not over what she is saying at this point; her anger over injustice is more generalized than that. She does not believe that Hy is responsible for the scenes she wants to depict, but Hy *is* responsible for something else, something that Glady Joe cannot entirely forgive. Glady Joe prefers stitching landscapes and monuments. People can hurt you, betray you. People are dangerous if you are not careful.

Sometimes in motel rooms between their children's homes, Glady Joe and Hy drink whiskey and smoke a little reefer. It is their secret. They say it helps them sleep better in strange beds. They buy it from a grandchild in graduate school, a young woman named Finn Bennett-Dodd. Who has promised not to betray them to her parents or the other relatives. Finn understands that, more than the fact that pot is illegal, it upsets people when two elderly grandmothers indulge in this private ritual. "It's just so unseemly at our age," Hy says to Finn, tucking the grass-filled Baggy away in her makeup case. She kisses Finn's cheek, lays her cool hand on her granddaughter's arm for a moment, Hy's musky smell tinging the atmosphere of the room. "It's not safe for us," she continues. "When you're young" (she smiles at Finn) "what is exciting or rebellious or eccentric becomes senility or a lost grip in one's old age." Glady Joe and Hy choose not to risk it.

They drive the Chevy for two reasons. One, it is a reliable, roomy, well-made American car with plenty of space for luggage and the miscellaneous junk they pick up in the course of their travels. And, two, it is a "grandmother" car; it comforts their children to see their mothers in that old machine, just as it would disturb them to see their mothers passing a pipe (they converted one of James Dodd's old Comoys for this purpose—removed the stem and kept the bowl).

"I'm a people person," Hy has been heard to chirp from time to time. "I really get a kick out of them," to which Glady Joe would lift her eyes over the top of her newspaper to stare at her sister, saying, "Give it a rest, Hy." And Hy would give her sister a dismissive wave of her hand and say, "Don't mind Glady Joe. The grump."

What set their house apart from the others in the neighborhood were its odd back rooms; they were covered floor to ceiling with bits of glass, tile, shells, and china. Some beads here and there. All affixed to the walls. Even the indifferent observer could not help but recognize the painstaking effort this project required. It covered only the walls of the laundry room, back den, and part of the large kitchen—as if time or materials suddenly ran out. For all the artistry of the undertaking, the effect of these rooms was not pleasant; it was more fascinating and disturbing, as if something raw and private were unwittingly (or, perhaps, accusingly) revealed. Glady Joe scarcely took notice. (While visiting this summer, Finn quietly examines the walls, runs her hand over their jagged surfaces. She does not need to ask what it means. She is the grandchild who knows.)

To Hy, these walls were like an anathema; she routinely refused to do the laundry or use the den and only reluctantly had anything to do with the kitchen, and that was only because the walls remained unfinished. "Not a moment too soon," said Hy, shuddering.

When Glady Joe was ill recently, Hy even appealed to Anna to come out of retirement as their housekeeper to do the laundry. Anna took a deep, unhappy breath, muttered something about "some folks," but did it anyway. "I'm not doing it for you," Anna told Hy. Her own daughter, Marianna, did not approve and wanted to know why Hy could not do it herself. "She is able-bodied as far as I can see."

But Anna said to her daughter, "You don't know everything," and came and did the laundry until Glady Joe was up and around again. Not before Anna stood nose to nose with Hy and said, "If you hate these rooms, you have only yourself to blame." Then went about her work.

Arthur Cleary, Glady Joe's husband, died a few years after Hy's beloved James passed on. Glady Joe seemed scarcely to grieve at all, which unnerved many of the quilters. "So life goes on," was all Glady Joe said, and Anna would defend her, quietly saying, "No one knows how another person feels in private." Everyone in the circle suspected that Anna knew something the rest of them did not. Hy was protective and nervous around her sister, though they could still be seen walking around Grasse together or sitting on the porch during the long summer afternoons, undone by the heat and drinking iced whiskey drinks.

Glady Joe and Arthur Cleary had more of a truce than a marriage; somewhere in the seasonless landscape of their middle age they finally came to the conclusion that they were never meant to be lovers, despite the warmth of their friendship. For so long they kept a polite, kind distance from one another, trying and failing at physical intimacy, never quite making contact. It was as if they were stranded in a foreign country and not only were ignorant of the local language, but spoke different dialects of their own, native language. Using the same words, but ascribing different meanings.

There was no thought of divorce because, well, they rather liked each other. And there were the children to consider (evidence that they had really, really tried, hadn't they?). Frankly, their marriage took on a curious permutation following this discovery of their sad incompatibility, and it drew them closer. They simply shifted their expectations, made them more manageable or "realistic," as Glady Joe liked to say. They were almost always seen together and were socially popular because other married couples found it so inexplicably pleasant to be around them, to bask in the genuine affection and camaraderie of their company.

They would arrive at someone's house, sit close to each other on the sofa; sometimes share a gin and tonic rather than have drinks of their own. People remarked that if only they could have a marriage like the Clearys' they would gladly sacrifice some small thing. Just to see what it felt like, being married to someone of whom you were so wonderfully fond.

Late at night, Glady Joe and Arthur laughed at the remarks made by their friends earlier in the evening. "Do you really think they would want to be so like us if they knew the truth about our lives?" asked Arthur.

" 'Be careful what you wish for'—that's the saying, isn't it?" Glady Joe said with a smile as she removed the small amount of makeup she wore for these evenings together.

"Well, yes," said Arthur, running his hands through his still-thick hair. Sometimes—it almost felt like unholy vanity—he stared for long periods of time in the mirror, coming away with a sense of his own attractiveness: his figure broader than in his youth and certainly the slack of his jawline a product of his years, his hands not too terribly spotted, but the face still nice-looking, still curiously "boyish." *I've seen women looking at me,* he comments to himself.

Arthur rose, taking his Loafers in hand, and padded in his stocking feet toward the door, toward his bedroom. ("It's because of the snoring," they explain to anyone rude enough to ask; "I don't have to tell you," Glady Joe adds.) "Well, well," he said, kissed his wife good-night, added, "In case you have a heart attack before we next meet." Arthur and Glady Joe used to say that jokingly to each other in the early years of their marriage, instead of saying "Hey, where's my kiss?" or "Didn't you forget something?" The black humor of it appealed to them, but now that they were older, it often startled Glady Joe—both to hear it and to say it to Arthur.

"Sweetie," said Glady Joe, looking up at Arthur from her vanity, her hand lingering in his for a long moment. She looked into his face and was unexpectedly saddened by the thought of a life without him.

Despite their arrangement, Arthur still has flashes of desire for his wife. He thought it would pass entirely with the passing of his youth, that he would cease to want to hold her close or would be content with an affectionate but sexless friendship, that he would no longer want to give her pleasure. Oh, most of the time he was in agreement that theirs was an association of comrades and not lovers, but there were still those times when he would laugh at some funny thing she said to their friends or inadvertently funny thing she said to their children; or see her in those crappy gardening clothes that carried the subtle scent of cow dung, yanking weeds or tilling the soil; or maybe it would hit him as he watched her dressing for an evening out, anointing the hollow between her breasts with Shalimar before dropping her dress over her head (careful not to muss her hair), turning her back to him, saying, "Sweetie, come zip me up."

The unfairness of his desire for her was that it

would assail him at any random moment. Arthur punched his pillow and tossed in bed; he could not get comfortable or stop remembering the smell of Shalimar, so named for the garden at Taj Mahal— one lovesick husband's monument to his absent wife.

Arthur drove Hy to the hospital. James Dodd, her much adored husband, was ill with a wasting disease. First, he was confined to a wheelchair, joking and putting others at ease by explaining that it was "just a temporary thing," which it wasn't. He said it was "fairly easy to adjust to," which it wasn't. Especially in a place like Grasse, small and nonprogressive, the handicap reforms still away in the future. James told their friends that "these wheels make it easier for me to chase Hy around the house." Hy and James could be seen moving down Main Street, shopping or going for milk shakes. Sometimes Hy walked by his side; other times they stopped in the park, with Hy sitting on his lap, sucking the ice cream through a straw, her arm around his neck. During holidays they decorated his chair with silk maple leaves in autumn colors or skeletons or black cats or streamers of green crepe paper and holiday wreaths.

At New Year's, they invited Glady Joe and Arthur Cleary, Corrina and Jack Amurri, Dean and Em Reed, and the Richardses for a fancy sit-down dinner. "I requested that it be sit-down," said James. For dessert, they served something called swan dreams, which consisted of meringue "swans" swimming in a dish of liquid, buttery custard and sprinkled with gold glitter (some of which was shining in unexpected glints off the Dodds' happy faces).

But all this was before James was hospitalized. His disease remained quiet during the fall and winter holidays, then, as if it made its own New Year's resolution, continued its course in January, and James began to lose the use of his left hand. The worst aspect of this illness, besides the obvious fatal one, was that it systematically rendered his body useless, yet all his nerve endings remained intact and sensitive. He could feel but he could not move.

It was not long before he was confined to his bed and sometimes, as Hy sat close to him or lay beside him, she could hear him crying. "Hy," he wept, "I'm not ready—it's over too soon." Other days: "Jesus, I'm only fifty-two," a statement that struck her as both accusation and prayer. Hy refused to cry (in fact, her sorrow seemed to her so profound that it was deeper than tears), though Em Reed, one of the quilters, told her that if she didn't express her sadness it would make her "sick inside."

Now it was the beginning of an extremely hot summer, with people walking around Grasse and Bakersfield saying things like, "Yes, but it's a dry heat," as if that were supposed to make it somehow more bearable. Arthur would drive over to Hy's to find her at the curb like a child awaiting her mother or a playmate, her skirt pulled modestly around her ankles, her expression distracted and somehow sweet. He told her, "Just wait inside where it's cool—I'll come and get you," but she would shake her head and tell him, "I'm too restless to wait."

Which struck Arthur as decidedly illogical, but he said nothing.

Sometimes, as he sat beside her in the car, he would marvel at how alike she and Glady Joe were, physically. Out of the corner of his eye, he could almost mistake one for the other, but looked at straight on, he could see that Hy took a little more care with her appearance, was without the more conservative aspects of Glady Joe, was slightly more stylish. They seemed to be aging in exactly the same way and at roughly the same rate, their figures subtly thickening around the middle, their legs still "good."

Hy carried the scent of musk, moistened and released by her perspiration. The air-conditioning dried and cooled her perfumed skin, which Arthur admitted he found seductive. Which led to shame and guilt.

But he began to live for the days they spent driving to the hospital, her musky odor filling the car.

Hy hummed along with the radio, sometimes singing in a high voice that occasionally found its key, then promptly lost it. Songs with words like *"till then, my darling, until then"* or about *"someone's laugh that is the same"* or watching out the window as she sang about *"the thrill of being sheltered in your arms."*

"Don't they break your heart?" Arthur blurted out one day, listening to yet another toneless rendition of yet another torch song.

"Yes," she said, "as a matter of fact they do."

At the hospital, Hy sits near the window watching James sleep. He breathes loudly, with difficulty, and she wracks her brain to locate the genesis of the place where she now finds herself. When did these troubles begin? The doctors themselves have no understanding of this illness, though they have seen it before. They asked, *Have you ever been to a South Sea island? Had a blood transfusion? Swam freely in an area of questionable purity? Any family history of muscle or nerve disorders? Lived in any exotic locales?*

Only here, she answered, in Grasse, this California farm belt. She resisted the impulse to add, But I've always felt so out of place here, as if *this* were the location most foreign to my life. The strangest place I could have chosen.

Well, said the doctors, what about pesticides?

At which point she informed them that her husband was not now and never was a farmer; he was a man of finance.

Ah huh, they said.

She wanted to say, James and I thought of living elsewhere, places we visited, and fed each other strange culinary delicacies made from the organ meat of animals or almost unpronounceable leafy vegetables and herbs—unusual mixes of sweet and bitter with nuts and white roots. We sat in an English café, outside, only to be told later that it was a "pub garden." James passed wine from his mouth into mine. Christ, what awful wine the English drink. We were told not to drink our beer cold, but warm. In the Middle East we were kept from entering sacred monuments because our legs were bare; in Rome, we were again kept out because our shoulders and my head were uncovered. In northern Africa we smiled freely at strangers, only to be scolded in their native tongue at our American rudeness.

Still, we promised ourselves that we would return and live abroad, perhaps Europe or Africa, but we never did. We were so out of sync with the local customs, like drinking cold beer in England or not understanding the language in Morocco, that we thought, if we were going to be outsiders, then why not just settle down at home, in Grasse?

Hy smiles to herself as she recalls how she and James would discuss the local occurrences in Grasse or Bakersfield, with all the wonder of itinerant travelers who were only passing through and happened to find themselves here.

Hy brushes her hair from her forehead, catches a whiff of her perfume as it passes her face. James sighs in his sleep; his "good" hand moves at his side. He is nothing, she thinks, but a prisoner awaiting his own death. She has to lean close to him these days in order to hear him speak.

Suddenly, she jumps up from her chair. In the middle of all her drifting and meandering thoughts came this one: *I want him to die. I want this to be over and done with,* and she is even more surprised to realize that this declaration is not accompanied by compassion but by anger and impatience. She grabs her purse and rushes from the room. She cannot even kiss James good-bye; she does not have the right to stay in this room or touch him. She needs to be touched.

In the hallway she tries to get Glady Joe on the phone, but there is no answer and she ends up calling Arthur's office. He says, Of course I'll come and get you. Say, you aren't . . . James hasn't . . .

No, no, says Hy. Just come.

She yanks the car door open before Arthur has brought the car to a complete stop and hurls herself into the seat. Crosses her arms like an unhappy, disappointed teenager, then begins to weep with loud, unrestrained sobs and tears that seem to fall two at a time from each eye *(eyes like Glady Joe's,* thinks Arthur, *eyes like my wife's).* Her foot bangs against the underside of the glove compartment and she commands Arthur to "drive out of town and let me out."

"Hy," says Arthur, "let me take you home."

"No," she screams, "NO NO NO NO NO NO NO NO NO."

Arthur quickly cranks the wheel and heads toward the outskirts. He silently curses Glady Joe; they had an arrangement—Glady Joe would pick Hy up from the hospital—yet here he was.

"And don't even think about stopping until we are a million billion miles from here. Until we're out in the middle of goddamn nowhere."

"Hy," Arthur begins.

"Don't even try," she whispers hoarsely, "don't even try to comfort me or understand me or anything with me. Do it and I'll hate you until I die. I promise. I will despise you."

They find themselves on Highway 99, passing towns so small they are scarcely towns, and acres of fields, some planted soon to be harvested, some fallow. Hy's mascara stains her cheeks, leaves long rivulets of black from her eyes to her jawline. "Stop," she orders, as they reach a town called Sula that boasts a general store, coffee shop, gas station, and some sorry-looking rental cabins. As Hy reaches for the door handle to get out, Arthur puts his hand on her arm in restraint. Her head snaps toward him (he could swear her teeth were bared), with feral eyes and jaw muscles working, clenching and un-clenching.

Arthur quickly releases her arm, as if shocked by electricity. "I was only going to say that you might want to check your face before you go in." He is angry now. "Christ, I'm sorry."

Hy flips down the sun visor and begins fixing her face in the mirror.

"I'm sorry that James is sick, Hy. I know it's ter-rible, but you aren't the only one who is losing somebody. You aren't the only one who suffers."

Spitting on a tissue, Hy scrubs the black trails of her tears. She keeps her eye on her reflection and says nothing to Arthur.

"I don't know what you want me to do. I don't know what to say." He looks at his watch. "Look, I have to call Glady Joe," and storms out of the car.

He returns to find Hy drinking a soda from the bottle, eyes free of makeup traces and closed. She hands him the bottle and he, too, takes a long swal-low. "Arthur," she says as her head falls back against the top of the car seat, "I'm so very tired."

"I know, honey."

"Can we just lie down somewhere? Before we go back? If I could just get some sleep somewhere for a few minutes, I'll be fine. I'll be okay."

Arthur turns the key in the ignition and tells her to "relax—by the time we reach home, you'll have had a nice nap," but Hy shakes her head. "No," she tells him, "I can't sleep at home. I can't rest knowing we are heading back. Ah, find me a great, shady tree and leave me there. Just for a few minutes." She closes her eyes as he slowly pulls the car back to the road.

It's lucky that he and Glady Joe always keep that ratty old blanket in the trunk of the car. It looks even more pathetic lying underneath Hy, who is sleeping as if drugged: motionless, careless. Arthur lies beside her, looking up into the branches of this golden oak. They are in the middle of an isolated cluster of oaks that he located near the highway on the side of a grassy, sloping hill. Away from the sounds of traffic. Perspiration beads on Hy's forehead, wets the base of her throat, and intensifies her heavy perfumed odor, which is noticeable even outdoors. It is so goddamn hot and still. He wishes he had thought to buy another drink and contemplates leaving her there while he makes his way back to Sula for another soda. He'd be gone only a few minutes, but what if she awakened and found herself alone? The picture of Hy as she looks when she waits for him on the curb in front of her house crosses his mind and he imagines her waking up, her face flushed from sleep and heat, whimpering because he is gone and she doesn't know where. He knows she would cry a child's sad cry of abandonment and not a grown woman's anxious sob.

Arthur's hands feel sticky from the heat. Glady

Joe promised to check in on James tonight and asked if he and Hy were coming back later or what. Did they want to stay north for the night? But he said, No, no, they'd be back. As soon as he calmed her down.

He leans back on his elbows, bored with watching the oak leaves, dappled with sky. He turns back to Hy. Funny how she is a more dolled-up version of Glady Joe. Even stranger that neither sister impressed him as being raised in a small agricultural town like Grasse; they each carried some other quality associated with old money or extensive travel, or possessed some gene of refinement. Yes. The Refinement Gene. Maybe it is the clear beauty of their skin or their choice of clothing or the fact that their father is not a farmer.

Now Arthur is lost in the memory of Glady Joe and how pretty and smart she was when he first found her. A little too serious, he supposed, and not conventionally pretty (though he thought her beautiful). And she was fairly well read for never having been to college. Of course, he was a college graduate, but that was more his parents' doing than his own. Still, he was grateful. What caught his eye in regard to Glady Joe was her love of *Jane Eyre*. He loved *Jane Eyre*, too. Such great friends from the start, drawn to each other by a shared love of reading and ideas, and soon he forgave his parents for moving them to this godforsaken town outside Bakersfield so late in his teenage years, because Grasse gave him Glady Joe.

It is unlikely that he would have thought to return to Grasse once he went to college if he did not know and feel a strong attraction for Glady Joe Rubens. The older half of the Flower Girls, as they were often called.

He once asked Glady Joe if she wanted to live somewhere else, almost certain her answer would be something like "I can't wait to get out of this place," only she surprised him by saying, "Actually, I like living someplace where I don't feel quite comfortable or welcome because it goads me into traveling or reading. I guess you could say that Grasse brings out the urge to 'quest' in me. I'm not sure I'd have that if I lived elsewhere. Any other place I may love," she said. "I might become happy and complacent and altogether content and then where would I be?" She laid her hand flat on her chest. "I ask you, what sort of life would that be?" She struck him as so mysterious, this mix of autodidacticism and small-town loyalty. He thought if he could come to understand her that he could come to understand himself; the key to her was the key to him.

When they had slept together a few times during a six-month period, Arthur knew he loved her. Glady Joe was not the most artful girl he had ever been intimate with (not that there had been so many, he had to admit), and there were times when the result was more frustration than satisfaction. It was evident that she was trying to please him, but there was something withholding about her when they made love. Sometimes he fought with her. And Glady Joe would look at him with a confused, open look as if she did not know exactly what she had done but it must have been something awful or he wouldn't be so angry. Then he would take her in his arms and apologize. She said to him, "I don't think you understand the risk I take for you."

If I marry her, he thought, *she will change.* It wasn't as if every time they were together it was bad; maybe it was a matter of security regarding her own future.

Hy stirs in her sleep. Arthur wonders if she always looked this peaceful when she slept. Glady Joe never did. She was serious when awake and serious when she slept. As if she could just not stop thinking about and mulling over and considering and examining the various angles of her day, her life, her children, her marriage—who knew which thought kept her so preoccupied even in slumber.

Hy sleeps like a woman satisfied. Her limbs are loose and generous, expansively stretched. Hy sleeps as if she is casually reaching for something, while Glady Joe looks as if she already has that thing but is puzzling out the way in which to keep it with her always.

Hy at fifty has the bloom of young womanhood off her face, but she has another, equally attractive, quality.

Arthur feels compelled to kiss her mouth. As he bends toward her, barely touching her lips, she awakens, slides her arms around his neck, and pulls him close.

Of course, he thinks, she smells nothing like Glady Joe's garden scent of cut grass, flora, earth, and sky, but physically he can almost convince himself that he holds Glady Joe in his arms, so similar are their figures and lengths when held under his own body. The worn touch of the blanket against the backs of his hands as he laces his fingers through Hy's damp, messy hair reminds him of Glady Joe; her voice, deepened by love, sounds like Glady Joe. It was Glady Joe who complemented the rhythm of his lovemaking, held her cheek to his. The fullness of Hy's breasts and the spread of her hips recall Glady Joe. If he closes his eyes against the heat of the day beneath the golden oak, he can almost convince himself that it is his wife he holds in his arms.

After, seated beside each other, content, Arthur leans over to kiss Hy's throat and, working his way up to her ear, takes her dangling earring in his mouth, pulls it off. "What?" says Hy, tugging her naked earlobe between thumb and forefinger. Arthur opens his mouth, presenting the sparkling object on the soft red cushion of his tongue, as if it were a valuable gift borne up from his heart and not something so recently attached to her person.

The first thing that strikes Glady Joe when she sees Hy and Arthur that evening is the powerful smell of Hy's perfume in the house. It seems to drift and settle about the furniture, underneath chairs, relax in the corners of the rooms.

"Naturally, James asked after you," Glady Joe says, haltingly because she couldn't seem to concentrate, "hopes you are all right. I didn't say anything, really, just that you had to scoot out of town for something." Glady Joe's words drift off as she tries to focus on the distraction of her sister's scent. It is as if Hy's perfume has shape-shifted and is now a fourth entity in the room; as if the musk has somehow become personified. Glady Joe tells herself it is because Hy sits in such close proximity to her. But as she looks at her she sees that Hy's lips are slightly parted, as if to make a statement or form a question or speak along on top of Glady Joe's words. Hy's body leans forward, drawn to her sister, her hair out of place from the windy drive home. "Really," continues Glady Joe, "it wasn't that easy, explaining your departure. I thought I could say anything and James would accept it."

Hy reclines back in her chair, the tension gone slack for a moment. "Now why, Glady Joe, would you think that?"

Glady Joe cannot answer; her sister's musky scent feels like an oppressive weight on her chest, a pressure on her heart.

"For chrissake," Hy continues, "he's only sick, not stupid." A sound emits from her throat, somewhere between growl and chuckle—"Only fargone cancer patients have the luxury of being so drugged that they don't even know what year it is." She begins to cry softly. "My James doesn't even have that. My James."

Glady Joe is moved to take Hy in her arms and comfort her, but she stops, finds herself snapping instead, "Perhaps *you* made that mistake when you took off down the road with my husband." She is as shocked by what she has just said as she was to find herself unable to hold her weeping sister. At the mention of the word *husband*, Arthur suddenly comes to life in the room, where he is sitting some distance away from the sisters. Glady Joe finds it peculiar that Arthur appears to be linked with Hy and not herself. She shakes her head, until something else occurs to her. Rising from the chair, she stalks over to where he sits, grabs his arm, and thrusts it under her nose.

"Glady Joe," he says with an embarrassed, irritated laugh and tries to pull his arm away, though his wife will have none of that. Leaning into him, she sniffs him arm to shoulder, shoulder to hair. Holding herself tall, she contemptuously tosses his arm back at him, backs away from both Arthur and Hy, her eyes beginning to fill.

"I have to go and think for a minute," she says.

"Honey," says Arthur, extending his hand, which repulses Glady Joe, causes her to react as if it were some sort of danger to her, some sort of weapon— "it's not," he says—but Glady Joe raises her own hand and cries, "Shut up—not a word—not if you care for me at all," and leaves the room, only later that night recalling the last thing she saw before she left was Hy's hand at her throat and her odd look of satisfaction and regret.

Immediately after Glady Joe's realization in the living room, she found she could not tolerate being near Arthur; it was as if no amount of scrubbing could wrest Hy's musky odor from his skin. At first, Glady Joe thought it must be because he was still seeing her sister and the smell was being renewed regularly, but when he demanded that she "stop punishing" him, she knew that it was a onetime thing. Still, Glady Joe's head was full of it.

Oh, Arthur was brimming over with remorse that night—not actually denying what had happened—it would be too insulting to her if he had—but sidestepping the encounter entirely. It is so difficult to make apologies and promises ("I swear, this will never happen again") when the act itself—the transgression—cannot even be broached.

"Can't I come in? Can't we work this out?" he said as he stood in her bedroom doorway that night.

"Don't come in here, Arthur. I'm afraid of what I might do." And when he did not leave, but remained there, silent, she said, "Are you stupid? Can't you see that I don't want you here?" She said "I don't want you here" slowly, carefully, as if she were talking to a lesser or very young person.

"Glady—" he began, which caused her to turn and hurl a heavy silver-backed hand mirror at him.

"Whore!" she screamed. "Slut!" She cleared her vanity table of atomizer bottles, makeup jars, an inlaid rosewood box he had given her for their second Christmas. He dodged the beautiful box, which broke its spine against the wall behind him.

"Have you gone crazy?" he demanded as she circled the room, searching for more missiles to launch. She would not be quieted; her only answer to any of his questions, genuine or rhetorical, was the sailing through the air of some object. "Do you want to kill me?" he hissed, as if he did not want to disturb Anna sleeping downstairs. Glady Joe, amused by this silly notion of silence, dropped her hand, which held a small porcelain bowl, ready to hurl, and said, "Yes, actually, I do." Then threw the dish at him anyway.

"I'm sorry, so sorry," he began to repeat. "I don't know . . . I can't say . . . ," speaking in phrases and not sentences, and, as he began to cry, his shoulders heaving, standing still in the doorway, she said, "I hate you."

A few days later he took a new tack, appealing to her sense of reason. "Our marriage," he said. "You know how it's been with us." And used words like "lonely" or "a man's needs" and "be fair."

To which Glady Joe shot back, "I thought we were friends."

"We *are* friends."

"*Friends* don't betray each other," she screamed, scanning the living room for something to throw.

After remorse and reason came pragmatism, mentioning their long marriage and what it meant.

"You have changed what it meant. You promised, you promised to cherish me." She turned from him, her hip pressed against the kitchen sink, watching out the window, and said quietly, "Fuck what it meant."

He brought her flowers, armloads of gladiolus, which she left to dry out on the dining-room table saying, "These aren't my favorite flowers." And when he looked confused, she reminded him, "These are *your* favorite flowers. We are not the same person. Don't mix me up with you."

Once he took the offensive, accusing Glady Joe of "denying him," forcing him toward "another woman," which made her squeeze her eyes shut, the red rising to her face, saying, "Hy is not another woman—she is my sister."

"Don't you see?" he asked.

"See what?"

"It was the closest I could get to you."

Which registered somehow with Glady Joe, quieted her. Made her so silent it was frightening.

"What I don't understand," says Arthur to Glady Joe as she stands atop a small ladder in the laundry room, "is why you have never blamed Hy."

"What makes you think I don't?" She does not look at her husband, who leans against the wall with crossed arms, watching her painstakingly apply fragments of porcelain to the walls in intricate patterns.

"Because you still talk to her."

"I still talk to you, too." Glady Joe, unhappy with the shape of this particular piece, exchanges it in her box for another. Soon she will run out of shards from this broken bowl and will have to find something else—maybe those remnants from the vase she broke the second night of her fury at Arthur.

"This is really creepy, you know," says Arthur, jerking his chin in the direction of the wall that Glady Joe is decorating. "Couldn't you just toss that stuff out? Couldn't you just let Anna get rid of it?"

"Arthur," sighs Glady Joe, then repeats "Arthur," but says nothing more to him. She wants to say, Arthur, I am not the kind of person who throws away something because it is broken. I would not waste what could still be of use. (*Quilts are comprised of spare time as well as excess material.*)

She applies more glue to the back of a piece of glass, affixes it to the wall. Since she began this project, a week after the throwing frenzy, she has felt a sense of purpose and calm, as if this is the only way she can somehow go on with her life—transforming these pieces of junk, swept up from her bedroom and bathroom floors, into art. Anna whistled at the extent of the damage done over a couple of days. She bent over to clean up the mess that had once been figurines, vases, small dishes and bowls, picture frames, boxes, even the tiny clay animals Francie and Kayo had made in grade school—all of which had been laid to waste—these shattered markers of the Cleary marriage; their life together as one.

The walls began to look like three-dimensional Persian rugs. It took a good length of time to complete the laundry room, and Glady Joe ran out of materials. So she turned to bright bits of glass, beads, shells. Pieces of tile. Then made her move to the back den. She had not intended to go this far; actually, she did not know what to expect when she began the project, she only knew that it helped to hold her fractured life together. She was careful to close the door when the quilting circle met at her house. The women of the circle could sense a coolness between Hy and Glady Joe, but they thought it had something to do with James's illness and his nearness to death. If that can't affect your personality, they reasoned, nothing can.

When Hy visits, she stands outside the doors of these rooms, usually in a stance of her arms holding each other, in an embrace of self. She rarely says anything directly about the rooms—though Glady Joe occasionally wishes she would so she could lash out something hurtful at her, about her being responsible, and so on—instead, she takes on an air of concession.

Once Hy said, "It's just that the effect is so—" She searched for the correct word. "So *what*?" demanded Glady Joe. "I don't know," said Hy, "busy or aggressive or . . . I don't know." Dropped her eyes to the floor.

Years later, this is what Glady Joe will tell Finn as she walks beside her on the campus of the midwestern college Finn attends, while Hy naps in the soon-to-be-vacated apartment. Finn had just completed her spring term when her grandmother and great-aunt decided to visit. And, of course, there is the little matter of their pot supply.

Glady Joe is explaining what happened, all those years ago, when Finn's grandfather was dying and Glady Joe was crazy from betrayal and looking for blood.

"I decided," she says, "to go to the hospital and tell James about Hy and Arthur. May he rest in peace. I thought, I'll bring him ice cream—his favorite, pralines and cream, and he will look up, happy to see me, trusting (no one should be so trusting, I thought), and I will sit on the bed, take his still good hand . . . no, I will stand at the foot and look him in the eye . . . no, better to pull up a chair and say something like, 'James, you and I are so much alike. Foolish and trusting. I always liked you tremendously and I think my sister was fortunate to have you for a husband'—I thought, oh, god, what if he whispers in that difficult way of his that he loves Hy, too?—'but here's the thing—she isn't worthy of you. She cannot be trusted not to hurt those who trust her. I know she's a goddamn "people person," but maybe all that means is that you see them as some sort of highly evolved pets that you can love or abandon as you desire. She abandoned you, James. We are so joined by her; she abandoned us both.' "

"Jesus, Aunt Glady," says Finn.

"I thought, Let the man die enlightened. Let him carry this burden of knowledge beside me. I was crazy, Finn—I would've done anything.

"But when I got to the hospital, with the pralines and cream, I looked in to see Hy curled in bed beside James—they really did adore one another, you know, your grandparents—she was stroking his cheek and whispering, 'You were always so clean-shaven during our marriage, so properly groomed, but I rather like you like this. So bohemian. I always thought you had the itch to be bohemian.'

"James's words were soft because the disease affected his lung and throat muscles. 'I'm sorry, honey,' I heard him say.

" 'Don't be sorry,' she said. 'Don't ever be sorry. It is pointless. I don't want to talk about regret. I want to tell you how I love you.' And I got to thinking of something I read somewhere which said that, after everything in our lives—after all we do or say or hope for—all that will be left finally, is love.

"There I was, eavesdropping in the hall, only partially recovered from what had happened between Hy and Arthur, still a little crazy—but I knew I could not do it. I could not. I came to hate myself for thinking that I could. I came to understand that betrayal cuts both ways. It would not have changed anything and, besides, I thought of what Hy was going through and the loss she was feeling and how I felt when I found out about her and Arthur and the loss I felt. And then there is the matter of blood.

"I stepped away from the door and walked down the corridor, even though the ice cream was melting. I needed to collect myself. Then I went back to his room, where we all ate from the carton, Hy spooning it into James's mouth since he could not do it for himself. I thought about family. I thought about forgiveness."

Glady Joe asks Finn if they can rest for a moment.

Sure, she tells her, knowing that she needs to ask about staying with them for the summer, something that she only this moment decided to do. Finds a bench where they can sit.

All this happened two weeks before James Dodd passed away. Before Glady Joe came into the room with the melting ice cream, James said to Hy, "Miss me?"

"Terribly," she answered.

"The hell of it," he said slowly, with great effort, "is that when you touch me like this, I can't touch you back. I can feel you but I can't touch you." He was exhausted by what he had just said.

Hy wanted to cry because she knew that what he described was how she would feel about him after he died—that she would live the rest of her life able to feel him, his presence in her life, but not touch him.

"Do you want me to adjust your feet?" she asked. James nodded.

"So irritating," he whispered.

Then she was startled by the sound of Glady Joe entering the room. Hy thought her sister looked like a woman with a purpose, and was suddenly afraid.

She watched Glady Joe lean into James to kiss him and receive a kiss. She saw her settle on the bed beside him. "My favorite," he said when she handed Hy a spoon for the ice cream. They began to chat easily, and Hy felt, was almost certain, that something had changed within her sister. It was as if something had been resolved or a fight resulted in a draw.

Earlier, when James had asked Hy if she missed him, she wanted to say, I've been missing you for months, and christ, life without you is so hard and empty and I have done a terrible thing, which is to take my sister's husband. I claimed him. I took him because you were being taken and no one asked me, so I took Arthur, unasked, and I know I'll never recover from the love I feel for you. I wish that I could talk to Glady Joe. I wish I could ask her why our lives are so brief when we still have so much love for each other. Sometimes I envy those old married couples who never talk or touch and really don't care much for each other's company, because I know they won't feel this severing, this unhappiness. It seems that our love should sustain us, instead of killing me, which is all loving you is doing for me now. Glady Joe once told me that we seek people we love in this life so after death we can be transformed into a surge of light and attract to us other particles of light, which are the essence of those people we loved on earth.

But Hy said nothing; says nothing—not to James or to Glady Joe, who is eating ice cream, leisurely, unhurried. Who, in return, says nothing to Hy of any significance, nor to James.

Instructions No. 2

IF YOU QUILT ALONE, CHOOSE YOUR SUBJECT CARE-
fully. Expect to live with it for approximately two
years, depending on the simplicity or complexity of
the work. The fairly intricate quilt will contain,
roughly, thirty-five pieces per block. Perhaps a
thousand pieces in the finished quilt. Shake your
head in amazement at the occasional quilt that
boasts *thousands* of pieces. Puzzle out the fact that a
single woman could hold all those pieces together
without misplacing, losing, or mistaking a piece.
Understand that she must be someone of extraordinary strength and organization and discipline. Someone who is a stranger to the false step in
life; someone a mother would admire. Question
whether you would share your mother's admiration.

The 1933 Sears, Roebuck Quilt Contest boasted
an accumulated cash prize of $7,500; $1,200 for the
first-prize winner alone. Manna in the thirties.
Shoes for the children. Rent paid up; food to eat.
Pressure off your husband for a few months, only
until the country turns that fabled corner and rights
itself. Read where the judges received 24,878 en-

tries. Do a quick calculation of time and cloth pieces. Understand the sum to be breathtaking: hundreds of years of time spent quilting millions of pieces. How to keep it all in order. Under control.

It is not simply the color and design, but the intricate stitchwork involved. Miles of small, perfect stitches, uniform, each as the smallest link in the overall pattern of beauty and grace. All hand-sewn, with the Singer machine idle by the wall. You know quilters. Boggles the mind. Forces you to sit down at your kitchen table, eyes closed, hand to your forehead, crushed under the weight of all those numbers.

Send away for a quilt kit from *Good Housekeeping*. Something with a complete scene as opposed to a repeating pattern. Perhaps a large house set back on grassy acreage. Fill it with children and a husband. Close your eyes and imagine the smells of cooked food wafting from the kitchen. Roast chicken and rosemary potatoes. Chocolate cake for dessert. A canary in the window that sings on command. The trees in the garden are lemon, peach, and orange. Bicycles near the garage; workshed containing your husband's tools and workbench. Clouds in the blue sky (be sure to place extra stuffing in the clouds for effect); eating outside at the redwood table. We all love each other.

Or picture a body of deep-blue water in the South Pacific. The figure of a woman poised to dive from a small cliff fringed by a rain forest. The palm frond made from embroidery silk, the water of satin. Yours and you lover's skin brown from the sun. The scenic, pictorial quilt is finite, contained.

You prefer it.

Contemplate crumpling the paper pattern of the pictorial quilt. A pattern, by its very nature, should repeat. It is your nature as well. To do as your mother did. As much as you hate it, as much as it grieves you.

The scenic pattern is the great dream; the repeating pattern a nod to reality. Your life. Everyone's life. Which brings you to the *Crazy Quilt* and its lack of order, its randomness, its shrouded personal meanings. Differentiated from a quilt with one theme; this other quilt that requires many hands, many meanings juxtaposed with each other.

Experience discomfort at the thought.

Consider the *Crazy Quilt*. Deplore its lack of skill and finesse. Express this idea to the women in your quilting circle. Say those words: lack of skill and finesse. Explain that this nineteenth-century fad is not translatable to the twentieth century. Insist that you are all modern women who control their lives and are not, in turn, controlled by them. Glower from your chair when someone laughs at what you have just said. Calls you silly; even though the tone is affectionate, you still feel put out. Concede the project.

Hold your secret regarding this quilt. What upsets you. What puts you out. Your inner conflict regarding the vagaries of control.

Read *The Story of O*. Convince yourself that it was, in fact, written by a woman or someone who thinks like a woman. Feel shame and pleasure at being forced to read it in the utmost privacy of your life. Wish you could talk to one of the other women about it. But you cannot. Dare not mention it; deny all knowledge of it should anyone else bring it up, even in a casual way. It is a novel of choices in a world of limited choices. On one level. You understand that concept. Remind yourself that, of course, her story is pure pornography.

The cradle quilt is a quilt reduced to infant or child proportions. The theme should reflect the child's immediate world: bow ties, balloons, trucks, buttons, lambs, and shoes. Incorporate an image a child can unconsciously think about; influence your child's dream state. Design a body of water. Surround it with rocks and trees. A bird or two would add "movement." Clouds fill the sky in great white billows. Again, puff them up with extra stuffing lodged between the appliqué and quilt top. Give them dimension. Get across an idea of summer.

Follow your parents' footsteps. This is what quilting is about: something handed down—skill, the work itself. Hold it in your hand. Fondle it. Know in your heart that you long to rebel; look for ways in which you are different from your mother; know that you see her in yourself at your worst times. Laugh as you contemplate the concept of free will, individuality.

Now think about the perfect marriage or the ideal lover union. It is as uncommon as any wondrous thing. Yet everyone *expects* to find it in her life, thinks it will happen (just a matter of time), feels entitled. Sit with the other women and express confusion as to why a mutual friend, so deserving of love, is living without it. Think of a million reasons as to why this is so, except the true reason, which is that it is an unusual and singular thing, having nothing to do with personality or worth. If it was so commonplace, why would artists find themselves obsessed by it, churning out sad paintings and torch songs?

As the twentieth century draws to a close, heads shake at the high divorce rate, the brutalization of the love affair, left in neglect or disarray. Leave that old lover. Move on. Take the A train. But in the dark of your room you may be moved to admit to yourself that you only *thought* you fell out of love or grew tired of it (grew tired of a small miracle of the heart?), when in reality you may not have felt love at all, but something entirely different. Once you love, you cannot take it back, cannot undo it; what you felt may have changed, shifted slightly, yet still remains love. You still feel—though very small—the not-altogether-unpleasant shock of soul recognition for that person. To your dismay. To your embarrassment. This, you keep to yourself.

Why are old lovers able to become friends? Two reasons: They never truly loved each other or they love each other still.

Sophia Darling

WHEN PRESTON RICHARDS FIRST LAYS EYES ON SOPHIA Darling, his future bride, this is what he sees: a young girl of seventeen walking purposefully toward a ladder leading to a high dive at the public swimming pool. He watches her move on her heels with an awkward grace, sounds of wet slapping flesh on the concrete, since she only recently emerged from the water. He notes the way she spreads her hands and flattens her dark, wet hair against her nicely shaped skull, then moves quickly downward to tug at the legs of her swimsuit; then back to her face as she clips the tip of her nose between her fingers, removing any lingering drops.

She is entirely unaware of these minor adjustments, ignorant of the ritual she performs each time she leaves the water and prepares to dive, but Preston Richards has watched her for three dives now and can discern the emerging patterns of motion.

He admires the tensile beauty of her long thighs, the flex of the muscle as she balances her body, her toes gripping the edge of the board—all concentration and potential motion. Her arms are suspended

55

for a moment straight out in front, away from her chest, frozen; then, as if some inner mechanism clicks, she strikes her hands out to the sides (like wings) then up, and in one smooth movement, she is airborne.

The pool is located in a town called Grasse, just north of Bakersfield proper. Today it is so hot, at least 99 degrees, though everyone is guessing in the lower numbers. This is how it is in these summer farmlands with the inhabitants wanting to believe that the day is not as unbearable as it feels. As if temperature is only a state of mind that can be controlled and willed to obey by holding a good thought.

Preston ceases to be aware of the noisy swimming-pool chatter, punctuated by the splashing and quarreling of children—the establishment of water-game rules or a child with closed eyes swimming blindly toward the other children, calling "Marco" as they answer "Polo."

Or the young mothers, their bodies teetering between that young-girl softness and womanly weight gain, talking and confiding among themselves. All of this falls away from Preston's consciousness as he watches Sophia fall into the water.

Preston Richards is like many of the men here today, men who work in town and who have stopped by on their lunch hour for a fast dip in the pool, just to take the edge off this thick heat. Preston himself has stepped away from his office— where he has been recording the results of the many soil samples he has collected for the company that is employing him for the summer—to try and cool his body in this sweltering weather. To his good fortune, he finds himself observing this slim, muscular young woman and wanting nothing more than to place his mouth upon her body, maybe sink his teeth into that powerful thigh.

Sophia Darling positions herself on the tip of the diving board, turns her back to the pool, freezes, then leaps. She twists in the air as Preston feels something within his chest rent ever so slightly. So astonished is he at this sudden weakness of his inner fiber, that he momentarily loses his concentration on the diving girl.

His hand involuntarily moves to his smooth chest.

Heartburn? Heatstroke? He tells himself that he should jump back into the pool, bring his body temperature down a notch. This tearing in his chest is curious because it makes him feel vulnerable, mortal, and he does not know why since it is probably the result of this hellish day or something he should not have eaten. He forgets Sophia (though years later he will say, "You jumped from a great height and flew into my heart"), pushes himself off his towel, and stands by the edge of the pool. As Preston hesitates, Sophia appears at his feet, her hands placed firmly on the concrete, pulls her body out of the water as it forms a clear, shining shell encasing her face and figure. *She is at my feet. She is rising to meet me.*

Without thinking, Preston crouches, hooks his hands beneath her arms, and lifts her high above the water's surface so that her hands lose their pavement anchor, her face startled and dripping. *How heavy she is*, Preston marvels. *So slim but how very strong and weighted*. And for a split second they are face-to-face.

Then her body twists free, sending Sophia to the concrete with a thump to her backside, her feet still playing in the water.

Preston wanted to pull her right up to his mouth, fresh from the water, to kiss her and kiss her with no thought of anything but the taste of chlorine on her lips, and all this because she leapt from a nine-foot-high dive and flew straight into his heart.

Sophia sits at the poolside, says, "Well!" then nothing.

Preston shyly drops beside her, apologizing, then, "I'm Preston Richards," extends his hand, so recently supporting her weight.

"Sophia," she answers, head tilted to one side, her gray eyes narrowing slightly as she looks over at him.

"Sophia what?"

"Darling," she says, then, "why are you blushing?" because Preston has nervously dropped his gaze, glances down at his hands.

"I don't blush," he says finally.

"Then," she says, her feet gently kicking under the water as she leans back on her elbows, "you are acting as if you should be."

This makes him laugh, says, "Actually, you are right. You made me shy for a minute there."

"Why?" She looks genuinely curious, as if she is about to discover something new about herself. Her wide smile reveals a gap between her upper front teeth. Though her eyes are squinting against the sunlight, she does not turn her face away from Preston's.

"Because I thought you called me darling," he tells her.

"Oh, god no," she laughs, closing her eyes and shifting her face toward the sun. "Oh, no, no. My last name. It's Darling. Like the family in *Peter Pan*." Her back arches, forces her belly upward, her head falling back so that her dark hair, in separate dripping clumps, almost touches the ground.

"Sophia Darling," Preston repeats to himself, barely audible, then louder, "I like that. I like that very much."

Sophia brings her head back up, the stomach tucks back in, and she is sitting, making whirlpools with her feet, hands folded in her lap. "Do you now," she says.

"When we are married, we will break tradition so you can keep your perfect name."

Her feet stop moving; in fact her entire body freezes. It is possible that she is hard put to even draw a breath. Preston recognizes this posture: It is identical to the moment when she stands poised on the diving board, before her body takes flight.

Sophia Darling says to Preston Richards: What I like about diving is the feeling of falling. Of the water rushing toward you and there is nothing to be done about it. You cannot alter your course once you jump from the board; you will land—without a doubt—it is only up to you whether it will be a smooth or rough landing. She thinks for a minute.

I guess you could say it combines certainty and the unexpected, she adds.

Preston wants to know if she dives competitively, "in school," for example, but Sophia shakes her head and answers, No, I just do it for myself. And when he inquires as to what she would like to do with the rest of her life, she says, smiling, "Marry you, I guess."

In that case, he says, matching her smile (already a little smitten with the space between her teeth), I better ask you out.

"A college man," said Sophia's mother with relish when Sophia told her about Preston Richards. "I've always wanted a college man. But listen, sweetheart, let him do all the talking. Men love a good listener; it makes them feel important and smart. Be bright, but not too bright, and let him see that you are a young lady, a girl to be respected." She paused as if trying to remember something. "Follow his lead or, at least, give the appearance of following his lead. Just to be on the safe side—men are funny that way."

"I'm not marrying him," said Sophia. "He's only taking me out."

"You never know if he is The One."

"Mother," sighed Sophia.

"You know I love you but you are not pretty enough to be on your own in this world," and before Sophia could open her mouth, her mother placed her hand in the air like a crossing guard stopping traffic: "I know whereof I speak."

At other times she said things like: *Sophia sweet-*

heart, marriage is a difficult undertaking at best and the secret is to please your husband and be there for your children. Do not wander from the path you have chosen.

Or: *Rule the house with a velvet glove that serves to hide your will. Make your husband respect you.*

And: *All else is failure.*

Mrs. Darling's love-advice often left her daughter ill tempered and suspicious and lusting after rebellion. More often than not, her mother's words forced Sophia from the house to the quarry reservoir, where she swam with fierce, cutting strokes. How could she make her mother understand that she might not want to "settle down" or that she felt a keen pleasure in the pure and unadorned sense of being alone? Then there were the days, trapped in the house with her mother's loneliness, that made Sophia wild to be married, to belong to someone. To love and be loved. And so afraid that it might never happen to her at all.

Her own father was long gone, having deserted Sophia and her mother during the Great Depression. She wonders what their lives would have been like had he not left. Whenever she asked her mother, "Why isn't Daddy here with us?" her mother would study her cuticles or brush imaginary wrinkles from her skirt and say, "Because I did not heed my own advice, the advice I give you." But Sophia remained suspicious, unconvinced that this was the path to being a successful woman—a *wife*—for how could a man desire such behavior from his girl? But then, one could ask, How could he not want someone so compliant? But she does not want to be like her mother, a woman who misplaces men.

She can barely recall the man who fathered her, yet she feels his absence most profoundly. Recalls him tucking her in bed at night and singing to her "Bye, Bye, Blackbird" or "Pennies from Heaven." Maybe an obscure Italian love song. Mrs. Darling insisted that Sophia was far too young to hold any memories of this man ("This wandering man," she said), yet she does, and it frightens her to think maybe she is like him in some way; maybe she is a wanderer, too.

She suspects that her mother was at fault in his defection; then again, she wonders if he was simply incapable of supplying the extraordinary amount of love required to nurture a wife and child.

Sophia cannot shake off her mother's touch, could not say to her mother, No, but that is not the life I want to live. She could not. This was because she was conditioned by life without her father coupled with the longing she felt for him; not a day passed that did not include a jagged awareness of his memory. It was her pilot and her compass; it broke her young heart—not all at once, in one great *crack!* but, rather, with tiny little fissures and hairline fractures. It chipped away at the perimeter as well, leaving her with a heart that did not have a smooth, voluptuous silhouette but one that was beveled and sharp.

If you took Sophia's heart and turned it upside down it would resemble nothing so much as a badly made arrowhead, one that lacked the stem to lash it to the arrow, but still had a point capable of piercing flesh.

Poor Sophia. Truly the progeny of her parents: the woman who stayed and the man who walked away. Poor Sophia, who is afraid to become like her mother, who misses a father she barely knew. So she wills herself to fall from great heights in an effort to understand her dangerous heart.

When Preston Richards comes to pick Sophia Darling up for their date, it is still quite light outside and the summer heat has only slightly subsided. She feels uncomfortable and silly wearing makeup, certain that the perspiration on her face will cause it all to streak unattractively.

Mrs. Darling is simpering and (Sophia is horrified) *flirting* with Preston. He grins and goes along with her mother to the point that Sophia wants to suggest that the two of them go out on this date. Let her mother look all made up like some strange doll face.

Her dress, too, gives Sophia a trussed-up feeling, cinched about the waist, snug in the bust. Thank god the war doesn't allow her to be wearing stockings or she'd have even more underwear on in this cruel heat. Inhumane.

After they have left Mrs. Darling smiling in the doorway of the house, it takes Sophia exactly two minutes to say, "Let's go to the quarry."

"My favorite song," says Sophia to Preston as they pick their way along the trail to the quarry, "is

'You'd Be So Nice to Come Home To.' I like Frank Sinatra a lot, too."

"I'm a Miller fan myself. He's the best," Preston tells her. "Makes me want to dance." He pushes aside a branch, waits for Sophia to pass safely. "Do you like to dance?"

"I do, but I'm not very graceful."

Preston remembers her long, muscular thighs, now covered by the skirt of her dress, and cannot imagine Sophia lacking physical grace. He wants very much to hold her in his arms on a crowded dance floor and tells her, "Then you haven't had the right partner."

"Is that so?"

"Absolutely."

As Sophia leads him through a seemingly impenetrable wall of leaves, which opens to reveal the quarry, he says, "Hey, you didn't tell me this was a swimming place." The still water is cradled by cliff rocks worn slick and smooth.

"The *best* swimming place," she corrects him. "As a matter of fact, I seldom go to the pool. You were lucky to catch me there yesterday. I mostly come here."

"I love it," he says without facing her. "This place looks like you."

Sophia openly stares at Preston, marveling at his comment. It is as if she makes some split decision, and says, "Okay, stay there and don't move." Preston watches as Sophia strips off her dress, kicks off her shoes, leaving her barefoot and in her underwear. "Don't follow me," she says over her shoulder as she begins making her way around the lip of rock surrounding the filled quarry. She moves with an athletic naturalness, surefooted and (he notes) she is smoothing back her hair with both hands, clipping the tip of her nose and tugging at the legs of her panties, as if she has just emerged from the water. He sees her hands go out to her sides like a high-wire walker and he imagines the rock narrowing, then widening, as her arms drop to her sides and her stride becomes more relaxed, less consciously balanced. Now the relatively small creature that is Sophia perches herself on the edge of a cliff about fifteen feet high. The dusk gathers as she ceases all movement, then, click, her arms swing to the side and up and she leaps. Her body knifes into the dark-gray water (the color of her eyes, he notes).

He wants to applaud, she looks so pretty.

Suddenly, he is afraid she won't surface, that she has met with some freak accident there below in the dark water, and he becomes frantic. Tearing off his shoes, he jumps fully clothed into the water, only to see her shining head bob up. Preston rushes toward her with a great deal of splashing and holds her tightly in his arms. He pushes her back against the rock from which she has only recently dived, supporting her with one arm as he cups her chin with his other hand; but not before she smiles at him, exposing the gap between her front teeth, which he briefly fills with his tongue before kissing her.

The earth, as Preston would say, occasionally resembles an extraterrestrial location or two. Just look at the Sahara or, if you wish to remain closer to

home, Death Valley. The sand beneath his feet in
the high California desert of Joshua Tree feels like
lunar dust. And only someone lacking all imagination could fail to see how easily the red moonscape
of the painted Sonoran Desert could be taken for
Mars. And since the earth contains many of these
odd plains, one only has to perform a quick leap of
the mind to see that to travel the world studying
rocks is to stroll the galaxy.

Perhaps it is in this spirit that Preston whispers to
Sophia, as he holds her in the chilled water, about
an odd-shaped asteroid called Eros that orbits the
sun by falling over itself, end to end, being only fifteen miles long and five miles wide. Since it is relatively thin—four and a half miles thick—one could
walk to the edge and look into the night sky at the
stars and the heavens above and below. It would be
a good idea, he says, to grip the edge when looking
over the side.

He presses her flush against the stone wall with
his heavy, clothed body. Now he is running his
hand along the inside of her thighs, splitting her legs
apart, nestling his body between them. Sophia
thinks she will lose her breath forever, will drown
and not care, will always have this sensation of inner
heat and outer cold. He cradles her against the
quarry rock. She trembles in his arms. She knows
what she will say and without hesitation. Yes.

And all this is permitted because the quarry belongs to her.

Suddenly, she imagines walking with Preston
along Eros, the star-filled sky glittering all around
them as she tries to defy the mysterious drawing

power of looking over the edge. She knows her father would take a chance, take in the view as her mother lingered behind.

Preston is wringing out his shirt and pants. Sophia cannot look at him, though his boxer shorts are not that different from the swimsuit he was wearing yesterday as they sat at the pool. Her dress is back on, the water from her bra and panties bleeding through it, leaving large wet spots across her chest, hips, and stomach.

"If we sit here the air will dry us," says Preston.

"I just don't see how I can explain this to my mother."

"Look, if we are dry when we go back she won't know."

Sophia stares at him. "Are you kidding? Look at your clothes. Look at my face." He catches her eye, and for a moment neither one looks away.

"It'll be all right," he says. "Look." He picks up a cloudy piece of quartz, palms it in his hand. "This is all right angles and planes. If I were to break this quartz it would crack along a prescribed plane. It's called cleavage." He passes the quartz over to Sophia. Leaning back on his elbows, he continues, "That would be different from a fracture because a fracture is a random break. And parting is more like splitting twins apart."

As he lays out his clothes, he is reliving in his mind the moment of holding Sophia, her singular flavor when he kissed her. The fish smell of her lake-drenched skin. He watches her in the gathering shadows with her dirt-caked feet and water-mottled dress, overwhelmed with a desire to keep her with him always. *We hardly know each other,* he marvels. "Sophia Darling," he says as he leans down to touch her shoulder. "I won't forsake you."

She looks up, weighing his words, testing their strength as if they are a bridge to cross, and shakes her head. "You know nothing about me."

"You'd be so nice," he sings. *"You'd be paradise, to come home to and love."*

It was unexpected that Preston would sing to comfort her. She wonders if perhaps he is meant for her, that he came for her across the years of their lives, to compensate for the loss of her father, and be the man who will stay.

Preston says this to Sophia "The sun was formed from broken stars. Our earth, its plants, and even us, are the product of the same clouds of gas and dust. You could say that we are born from stardust. He stops, then: One more thing about partings; no two are alike."

Their clothes dry, Preston hoists her in his arms (her dress falling back to expose her legs) and carries her back up the trail.

"Put me down," she laughs, "you'll hurt yourself." But he ignores her warnings, keeps her aloft. "Come *on,*" she insists, but he continues carrying her, singing "Stardust," "As Time Goes By," and "My Man," which he prefaces by saying, "I'll pretend I am you singing to me," and lifts his voice to a high girlish falsetto.

Sophia crosses her arms and grows silent. "You'll put your back out."

"Light as a feather, baby, you are."

"Then why are you puffing and sweating?"

"Because I'm a man." The word *man* comes out deep and resonant.

She laughs.

"Now," he sings, *"I am only going to sing my conversation to you for the rest of the evening."*

So for the remainder of their trip back to the car, Preston sings all his questions and answers to Sophia, who responds by taking his face in her hands and kissing his mouth. *"Feel free to join me,"* he sings at one point.

Sophia steps into the unlit house just ahead of Preston. Her mother sits waiting in the dark living room. As Sophia turns on the light, Mrs. Darling's glance misses nothing, from the absence of makeup on her daughter's face to the rumpled condition of Preston's clothes. The brush of his hand across Sophia's. All she says is "Do you love my daughter?"

"No," Sophia answers quickly, while Preston's voice smothers hers with his own reply. "Actually, Mrs. Darling, I do," causing Sophia to state again, emphatically, No!

Mrs. Darling sighs, slouches in her chair, and muses—to herself exclusively, it seems—"Then what is to be done?" It is not really so much a question as a meditation. "You aren't from around here, are you?" asks Mrs. Darling.

"No," replies Preston. "I'm still in college in Arizona. But I can take her with me."

Mrs. Darling turns from the couple and gazes out

the darkened window into the Grasse night, then looks back in anger. "Is that supposed to comfort me? That you'll take my only child?" There is an odd sort of amazement in her voice. "I shall be left." Her fist goes to her mouth. "I shall be alone."

"I love her," is all Preston can say. Then, "I think I may even need her."

Of course, Sophia has not yet graduated from high school and Preston needs to complete his degree at the school in Arizona. Though Sophia will miss having him sing to her, she is not altogether unhappy at his departure.

Ever since their visit to the quarry she has stopped going there, preferring to swim in the public pool. She tells herself it is because she likes the crowds; she tells herself that the memory of that day and her longing for Preston becomes more acute at the quarry. Besides, the pool belongs to everybody. But it is more than that. The quarry was her secret place. Why had she brought him? To allow him to see her in her entirety.

She remembers the way she trembled in his embrace.

More than anything she wanted to tell him that her life wish is to travel the world with him, swimming in the various bodies of water marking the world, floating on her back in the Dead Sea, splashing through the Mediterranean waves. Or chill to the crisp coolness of the northern Pacific; shift for hours in the warm blue of the Hawaiian Pacific. Dive in the South Seas. The aqua Caribbean, Smith

River, tributaries, and possibly rinse her face with water from an icy fjord.

She will swim and her husband will study the shifts of the moody earth; he will examine the chalky Dover cliffs, arid red-gold mesas, note the striations of sunbaked seaside hills that have been pushed by tectonic plates into powerful arcs of layered rock. He will collect geodes, so ugly from the outside, so gorgeous inside. Granite, schist, gneiss, rose quartz, mica, olivine, bloodstone, obsidian. Volcanic rock. Water wears away stone; earth to ocean. And he will present her with his finds, from his hand to hers (as he had that day at the quarry), showing her what it is that he sees. Sophia will grow stronger and leaner, swimming and diving, with Preston by her side, in this marriage of basic elements found in nature.

But somehow it all backfired on her, leaving her with a feeling of having muddied something that was once clear and pure inside her. She wanted him to see her dive from sheer rock face; she wanted to show him the sort of possibilities she embodied, but in the process she neglected to tell him this fundamental thing about herself. She allowed him access to her body without revealing what was in her heart.

This is what life is like on Eros, she thinks—never knowing when you have ventured too close to the edge, lost in a dream of the view of the sparkling heavens and never of the danger.

Does she love Preston? She can barely bring herself to ask.

* * *

The world's first known irrigation system was around 3000 B.C. in India and Egypt. And there are various kinds of irrigation, depending on the chosen crop. No knowledgeable farmer would water a rice crop the same way he would a citrus grove: Rice fields are meant to be flooded, whereas the citrus grove has greater success with a sprinkling system. There is the soil-to-water capacity, which must be taken into consideration.

Water is king in the California farmlands.

Some of the produce grown around Grasse includes cotton, grapes, alfalfa, potatoes. But there is another type of field that is equally important to Kern County; the oil field, with its derrick rising from the soil like a shunt to coax the earth's fossil fuel to the surface.

This watery world, where the oceans cover more of its surface than the landmasses, where, with the exception of the earth's core, all else is moving, shifting fluids. Even the continents float on currents of liquefied rock.

Sophia and Em are fishing in the subirrigation ditch. It is not the most scenic place in which to spend the better part of the day, yet here they are. They know there are better fishing spots, but they come here on occasion, as they have since they were children. The trees they recline beneath and the hats they wear provide little relief from the sun, and Sophia resists the urge to jump into the water; no sane person would venture into this standing ditch water.

Em is telling Sophia that she is a lucky girl to be going out with Preston Richards, who has two very nice things going for him: He is not away in the Pacific fighting the war, and he is not from around here. "Do you know what that means, Soph? It means you might actually leave Grasse. You might marry him and leave this place."

"You and my mother," says Sophia, "have marriage on the brain."

"So?"

"I'm not sure it is enough."

"Enough what?" Em leans her elbows on her knees but looks over at her friend.

"Adventure. Maybe. Or love or happiness or . . ." She laughs. "Or maybe I just want to take a tramp steamer to Hong Kong and drink Singapore slings."

Em reels in her line, replaces the bait ("I thought I felt something"), and lifts her sunglasses from the bridge of her small nose to wipe away the perspiration. "Then why take up with him?"

A certain earnest quality enters Sophia's voice. "Listen, I think he's different; I think if I could have the life I want I could have it with Preston." She hesitates. "I don't really want to marry. Ever. And Preston, well, when I think about him as a husband all I can see is myself as a wife." She gazes across the water, looks to the endless fields. "I don't know what I am saying."

"I think if you let him get away, you'll be sorry. Be thankful that he'll get you out of town."

"Yes," says Sophia quietly, "I am in need of rescue." But suddenly Sophia feels a chill and hears an echo of her mother's voice and she is momentarily afraid that she has just invited her own bad luck and that she will find herself old and unmarried and enormously sad. "I do want to marry," she finds herself saying. "You get married. You have children." Her words almost sound like a recitation. They have that quality.

"Children," says Em, smiling, "lots of kids."

"Children," continues Sophia, "and everything is great. Everything will be just great, won't it?"

"Check your line," says Em.

"He said I could be Darling."

"What?"

"When I met Preston he said I could keep my own name."

"Right," says Em, "as if you want to."

Sophia is again overwhelmed by the desire to leap into the water. To submerge herself, to purify herself. She imagines swimming down the irrigation ditch until it merges with a river, then spills into the ocean. Her stroke is even and perfect and strong. "I'm too hot for this," she sighs, setting the pole in the grass. "Let's go to the pool."

"You and that stupid pool," says Em, reeling in her line. She tears off the bait, then bites the line with her teeth, returning the hook to her small tackle box.

But Sophia is now lying motionless in the grass, her hat over her face.

In Arizona, Preston recalls the moment he held Sophia in his arms, slippery and almost mythical, finally fulfilling his primary impulse upon seeing her that day at the swimming pool, his willingness complete when he felt her shiver in his arms. It was then that he discovered the imperative of keeping her with him always.

As she stretched between his body and the stone he understood that a life of hunting rocks and minerals would be a cold, unyielding, and literally hard life if he did not have Sophia there to remain between himself and his vocation. A life without her would mean a life of falling into the bleak solitude of being a man with only his work to keep him company. Sophia would deliver him from his fate.

Sophia imagines that she could have told Em, as their fishing lines floated in that brackish water, that she is pregnant. It will be a scandal and her mother will cry and Em will stand by her, yet she says nothing. It is something she cannot discuss with anyone until she comes to grips with it herself. It means her transformation into somebody's wife (Preston's wife); it means settling down. It means trusting that Preston will come back to her once he, too, is told.

Her father's ghost looms up before her like a character in a German opera, his words resonant, beautiful, and dark. And she a child once again, hearing the Italian music of his voice, not understanding the language, though the meaning is implicit: All the words string together to let her know that he is leaving.

Sophia does not grow leaner and stronger (as she once thought she would, swimming the world over); she grows heavy. All this weight for that little Duff, their first daughter. Sophia watches the dream of her swimming moving away from her, never to be retrieved. She thinks for a moment of leaving both Preston and Duff, consoling herself that, no matter what happens, they will have each other. "Why," she says to herself, "I am no better than my father." She sits down, her hand resting lightly on sleeping Duff's head.

She is angry, too, and tells Preston that if she has to stay home with the child, so does he. She will not have him wandering the world, only to bring back his found treasures heaved up from the earth, to give to her as pale souvenirs. He will not travel the world and examine its faults.

"Sophia," he says, "are you trying to kill my research? My career?"

"Of course not," she tells him. "I'm only saying that if I have to stay, so do you."

"But it isn't as if you'll be alone. Your mother lives here. Be fair."

"Oh, please," says Sophia, "let's talk about something else."

"Honey," he says gently, "it isn't as if I am never coming back. I'm your husband. That means something, doesn't it? We have a child, we have a life." He holds both her hands in his.

"That doesn't mean anything," she says, "that because we are married you'll come back. Not a damn thing." He throws her hands back to her in disgust. "Ask my mother," she says as he leaves the room. "Ask me."

It is expected that Sophia will do as her mother did; this is the legacy of the time into which they are born. Sophia lives with the inheritance of her mother, who lived with the inheritance of her mother. She is not expected to attend to her own intrepid journeys or follow her own desires. Her time does not encourage it.

Sophia can gaze out her bedroom window and wonder what it was that prevented her from seeing the world, until her reverie is broken by the sound of her child calling out to her. Certainly she is aware of aviatrices and actresses, but she cannot count herself among their group; she is so much more ordinary than they even if her drive is similar.

How free she felt that day at the quarry with Preston! How so "like herself." In that one moment of physical, sexual freedom, where she gave herself over to him, she remembers feeling as if she were silencing the voice of her mother, putting to rest all the social expectations of a girl in her place. She laughs now (as she reluctantly moves from that bedroom window to see after her child), recalling the consequence of her actions—falling into the dark water, falling into Preston's embrace, inadvertently falling into the life she had been raised to live.

There was a day when Preston was back in Arizona mailing her letters of love, when she believed that their marriage would, in fact, be a wondrous thing—before she knew she was going to have Duff and still thought that she would not be a woman of her day, that she would join ranks with women who saw things and did things. And she would be with Preston.

But that turned out to be over before it began. Because: This was not a time when women could swim freely, unfettered by waiting domesticity; this was not their time.

She was only Sophia Darling. Sometimes she said that to herself as she enrolled the kids in special activities after school or involved herself with PTA fund-raisers or amassed the neglected possessions from neighbors for white-elephant sales. Or when she sat mute, quilting; she said to herself, *I am Sophia Darling. That is all.*

To be known as Mrs. Preston Richards was to exact a certain amount of social respect. She had gained entry into the ranks of motherhood with the birth of Duff. Even "the daughter of that poor Mrs. Darling," her mother's daughter, lent her a modest measure of communal visibility. These were all Sophia's identities and parts, the parts she grew to mistrust for her duplicitous feeling when she played them.

So to say *I am Sophia Darling; that is all* was, in this time and place, this homemaker era, to admit she was nobody.

Preston and Sophia have two more children after Duff, a son, Pres junior, and a daughter named Edie. Once a week, Em comes by and together she and Sophia walk over to Glady Joe Cleary's, where they quilt with six other women. It fills an evening normally spent not talking to Preston or talking to him through the children. Sophia waits for him to complain, to register some dissatisfaction with her, because she is ready to point out all the ways in which she is very nearly the perfect wife. Sometimes she thinks she only strives for this perfection so she can toss it up to him one night when he tries to engage her in one of his discussions about the State of Their Lives. When he tells her how unhappy he is doing soil samples for landowners around Grasse.

Occasionally, she can imagine him pushing down the desire inside himself to leave and see all those places they talked about so many years ago.

But if she makes herself so perfect, so unimpeachable in her behavior, he will be forced to stay, will have no legitimate reason to leave. It occurs to her that Preston is like her father in many ways.

There are times when Sophia wants to throw it all over, pack the kids in the car, and take off with Preston to all those places. See all those things she longs to see and fall in love all over again, as if love is not a finite thing but something fluid and changing, something that can ebb or surge like an ocean tide. Sophia wants to tell Preston that she loves him, wants to be less rule bound with her children; but instead she spends one night a week piecing together bits of fabric with a group of women. As if she could piece together all the things she feels inside, stitch them together and make everything seem whole and right.

When Duff is sixteen she tells Sophia she wants to go to college.

"Honey," says Sophia, "we cannot afford to send all of you and, besides, it is more important for Pres to go than you or Edie. When you are married you'll see what I mean."

(It is unusual for girls like Sophia's daughters to dream of college, given their isolation in Grasse and their era, which is 1950. But they are modern girls, despite their mother.)

Duff wishes she could tell her mother about her teenage years, but Sophia only sits with Duff and Edie, dreamy-eyed, wistful about the grandchildren they will give her. Duff says, "Mom, I'm not so sure that is what I want. I think there may be something else."

Which causes Sophia to freeze and say, "There is nothing else." Sophia, who has grown so skilled at heading off words she does not care to hear.

Duff, thinks Preston of his daughter, *Duff is great.* A little too serious and tense at times, but there is a quick intelligence there as well. He takes her to collect specimens, walks by her side. He gives Duff her own hand lens ruper to check the angles of various minerals. He instructs her in how to work the scale that assigns values of hardness to each mineral. Explains the difference between rocks and minerals. Illustrates with his palms the action of a lateral or a slip fault. Together they draw topographic maps and talk about half-lives and continental drift.

She can be very funny—not that Preston often laughs at her jokes; he does not know why this is except that it seems to be beyond him. When did he become a father and no longer Preston Richards? Preston, he thinks, would laugh at his comical daughter, but the Father cannot allow himself the luxury.

Pres, his son, looks so much like Sophia. The

same straight, lean figure and deep, gray eyes. He even inherited the space between her front teeth. But water holds no magic for his son; he enjoys swimming as a way of cooling off and nothing more. There is something Preston cannot quite identify in his boy—some independence of spirit that is held in reserve by his duty-bound nature. Pres junior worries about Sophia.

He heard them talking the other night after dinner as Sophia's hands dipped in and out of the dishwater, soaping the plates, then rinsing them beneath a steady stream of clean water. She passed them to Pres junior, who stood beside her, almost inarticulate because she was asking him about his college plans.

She said, "You do want to go to college, don't you?"

"Sure," he told her.

"Have you thought about where you'd like to go?"

"No. Yes. Maybe"—he appeared to concentrate on the task at hand; appeared to avoid Sophia's calm gray eyes—"back east or maybe down south. Somewhere, you know, somewhere else."

Sophia nodded. The front of her shirt was splattered with drops of water, as if she had been lying on her back in a summer shower.

"It isn't that I won't miss you," he said quickly.

"That never crossed my mind, honey."

"I mean, well, you have Dad. And Edie. And I'll be home for visits. You will hardly miss me? Right?"

Sophia released the water from the sink, listened

to it disappear down the drain. She smiled at her
son. "Such a funny boy you are."

Preston shakes his head at the conversation, for it
is the same thing when he and Pres discuss college.
His son is eager to go—far away, back east, down
south—but he cannot seem to talk about it without
asking over and over, "What about Mom? Will she
be all right, Dad? If I'm gone will she be okay?"

Preston has to laugh. "Pres, of course she'll be
fine. I'll still be here. God knows, I'm not going
anywhere." Which seems to reassure Pres, but only
until the next bout of worry assails him.

It is Edie who is most like Preston. *What does this
mean?* he wonders. *Who am I, what does being like me
mean?* He shakes his head: A romantic? A wanderer?
Surely he is neither of those, if he examines his life.
He was once someone who moved without thought
of the consequences, acted on nervy impulse. Like
his marriage to Sophia, his fishgirl, who adapted
herself to home and hearth with a vengeance, like
someone who has something to prove or a debt to
pay back.

It is Edie they should watch, Edie, who appears
so guileless and unconcealed. It is Edie who has the
potential to surprise.

Sophia does not enjoy the freedom of color and
pattern in the *Crazy Quilt*. The circle keeps talking
about making one, then rejects it for some other
project designed by Anna Neale. Sophia prefers the
challenge of a traditional, established pattern. That
is the true challenge, she thinks—to work within a

narrow confine. To accept what you cannot have; that from which you cannot deviate.

Em, now married to Dean Reed and with a daughter of her own, says to Sophia one evening as they walk to Glady Joe's to quilt, "How is Edie these days?"

"Good. How's Inez?"

"Inez," says Em of her own child, "is doing well. But Edie . . ." Her voice loses volume, deflates before she finishes her sentence.

They arrive at Glady Joe's and Sophia reminds herself to ask Em later, after the circle breaks, what she is trying to say about Edie.

Of course, Sophia forgets, and as she lies in bed next to Preston, pressing her brain to recall what it was about Em tonight in their conversation during their walk, finds that all she can remember is Em's breath hung like misty blue clouds in the cold night air.

"For you," says Preston, pulling Sophia by the hand into their backyard.

"Oh, Pres," she says. And there, before her, is a small pond that he had dug as a gift for her for their twenty-second anniversary.

"I thought you could wade in it or keep fish or whatever you want. I think it's deep enough."

So proud was he of his gift to her, so pleased when she sat by the small bank and cried into the palms of her open hands.

★ ★ ★

Around the time of Edie's sixteenth birthday, Sophia takes a long look at her as her daughter leans
on the open refrigerator door, orange-juice bottle
tilted to her lips, head thrown back. Sophia can see
Edie's throat muscles working, taking the liquid,
and she is about to say, *Honey, why must you always
wear that awful windbreaker,* when something else
catches her eye. Edie's slender frame has gone broad
around the middle, down a little low, the curve of
the belly unmistakable. "Oh!" exclaims Sophia,
which causes Edie to turn toward her, red-faced,
clumsily shoving the bottle back into the fridge, ad-
justing her windbreaker. Hastening her retreat.

"Look, Mom," she begins, "I didn't mean to
drink from the bottle," while Sophia can barely
speak. *How is Edie these days?*

She is trembling. Sophia says, "Edie," and cannot
finish her sentence, to which her daughter screams,
I said I was sorry, and rushes from the room.

Sophia slowly rises from the table, smooths back
her hair with both hands, her hair that was once
dark and shining but is now shot with coarse gray.
She tugs at her dress and clips the tip of her nose.
She ascends the stairs.

As Sophia looks in on Edie, who sits on her
bed, she says, "How could you let this happen?"
She does not say, Why didn't you tell me sooner?

"It wasn't only me," says Edie.

Sophia sighs, edges toward her youngest child,
her slim figure so like Sophia's at that age. "Let me
break it to your father, in my own way. I guess the
boy will have to marry you."

Edie, sad-eyed, looks away. "I don't know about that."

"Of course he'll marry you, honey," she says quietly, comfortingly. "It's not so bad. You'll see." She cannot be truly happy about this turn of events, yet she can find a way to accept them as inevitable. Her daughter will get married sooner or later and, after all, Sophia was only seventeen when she met Preston. Sophia runs her finger along the bedspread, sketching out the design for the beautiful crib quilt she will put together with the other quilters. Something with lambs and bunnies.

"That is not what I meant," says the girl. "I mean, I don't think I want him for a husband."

She cannot answer. She cannot make a crib quilt for a child without a proper name.

When Em whispers to Sophia one night at the quilting circle, "Surely you could reconsider the adoption," Sophia responds loudly by saying, "This is not your business, Em."

Then looks across the unfinished quilt they are working on to see Anna Neale coldly watching her.

Preston sits with Sophia out by the little pond that she never uses. She is saying that they should send Edie to a home in Colorado to have her baby, then bring her back to finish school.

But Preston only says, "How could you give away a child of ours?"

"Pres, it's not our child. It is Edie's child."

"But Edie's our child," he insists.

"Yes."

"I don't understand you, Sophia."

"What don't you understand? I'll tell you what: If she would marry the boy, I would feel differently, but she refuses. I won't have a child in my house raising her child without the *sanctity* of marriage. Yes, marriage. Grown-up responsibilities. Wouldn't it be nice if we could all just follow our heart's desires?"

Preston has remained silent. "She's our daughter. I will miss her."

"And I won't?" Sophia splashes her hand roughly in the pond's dark water. "Why is it always that everyone else is supposed to get what they want?" It almost shocks her, this mother's role, her mother's voice emerging from her mouth with such conviction. This role she essentially mistrusts; the role she cannot quite abandon.

"Why don't you ever use this pool?" asks Preston.

"I'm busy. You know that."

He nods his head. "Remember when you took me to the quarry? I've never known why we stopped. Why you stopped."

Sophia shrugs her shoulders. "I don't know. When I became a wife and mother, I guess."

The picture of Sophia leaping from the quarry rock slices through his memory, and he wants to cry out, to tell her he loves her and has missed that about her. Instead he agrees to investigate sending Edie to Colorado for the duration of her pregnancy. He rises. He passes his wife without touching her and goes to find Edie.

* * *

It is almost impossible for a mother to separate the reality of her child from the abstract idea of her child, and some women never do this at all. When Duff was an abstract idea, Sophia's first thought was that she wished her gone; her impulse was to erase the pregnancy. It was not a matter of wanting to "get rid" of it as much as wanting it to have never happened.

Then there was this child after nine long months and, suddenly, Duff was no longer an idea but a fact. There was no question of loving that girl. None at all. And, because of her circumstances prior to having her (that is, lusting after water and seeing in Preston someone who would take her to that water—or, less dreamily and more pragmatically, the fact of impending motherhood when she was unprepared for it), it was as if the pregnancy and the birth were truly two separate things that each had the power to open and close Sophia's world.

And it seemed to Sophia that the woman who cannot happily greet her baby from the very moment she becomes aware of its existence is a woman who will live in secrecy, hoping that no one (least of all the child, least of all Duff) ever suspects that she once wished it gone.

The phone call from Colorado came early in the morning: that Edie had run away in her ninth, dangerous month. She went to town to pick up something and never returned. Could one or both of them come at once?

Preston said that he would go and, curiously, Sophia was not overly worried about her child's escape; was she being ignorant or callous or trusting? Perhaps it was something she would have done herself. No, Sophia acknowledged, she was too much like her own mother to attempt such an action, but she knew she would have wanted to do it. Some things were so difficult to know, but she felt it possible that Edie would turn up at Duff's.

Duff, who has long since moved to Chicago, a childless, unmarried ("Christ, I've become a modern statistic, Mom") career woman. Sophia cannot help but imagine Duff in a smart suit, trading witticisms with William Powell or Cary Grant types; bright, feisty Duff. *I never could have been a career woman,* Sophia tells herself—*I mean, swimming isn't a career.* Perhaps Duff will find the right fellow; Sophia hopes to god she does, because a manless life is a lonely one; Sophia feels it most acutely since Preston has gone to find Edie and still has not come home. He has not even been heard from. Sophia does not even know where he is.

She lives with Pres junior, who attends the local college, and every time he mentions leaving, Sophia blanches and is silent.

Instructions No. 3

DO NOT UNDERESTIMATE THE IMPORTANCE OF THE carefully constructed border in the quilt. Its function is to keep the blocks apart while binding the entire work together both literally and thematically. But before you are ready with needle and thread, it is best to experiment with the layout of the blocks.

As you prepare to join your blocks, affix them to the dining-room wall or pin them to a set of drapes or arrange them upon the bed you share with your husband. You want to imagine how they will look once bound together. Think about what binds you to your husband and he to you. Marvel at the strength of that bond, which is both abstract and concrete, spiritual and legal.

A nineteenth-century Englishman said that marriages made in Heaven are subject to the will of the angel or the will of Heaven. And when a couple passes into the next world, they will become one angel. That is their fate, their destiny. This carries a certain appeal for you.

Consider the courtship of lovers. The way in which you imagined how the marriage would look before it took place. But perhaps you had other things on your mind before you tied the knot.

Think of how it all began with that first kiss.

Klimt's surrendering golden kiss that shimmered on the canvas. The kiss of reverence, of desire. The kiss of the wave as it slaps the shore. Neruda wrote, *In love you have loosed yourself like sea water; I can scarcely measure the sky's most precious eyes and I lean down to your mouth to kiss the earth.* Your sun-kissed garden. The kiss that first united your body to his.

Meditate on the soul-kiss, which, prior to the twentieth century, meant that the souls of lovers were exchanged; mouth to mouth, tongue to tongue; transferred from one to the other as a great gift and act of faith. But the body grows lonely for its old soul (even as it loves the new one) and longs to have it returned. A quilt, though stitched together, will always be separate, individual parts.

You understand this loneliness of giving a part of yourself away to the man to whom you are wed, the man who is sometimes called away, the man who is seldom home. Though the exchange of souls carries with it the promise of return.

Take special care when arranging your blocks; be sympathetic to harmonies of color, fabric, and form. Do not be hesitant in devising new, different ways to link the patches to each other; what works for one quilt may not be successful for another. Keep this in mind should you find yourself doubting your design.

Use only the highest-quality thread when piecing your quilt together. Remember, your intention is to make the quilt last forever. Traditionally, quilts are stitched with white thread, but if you feel the addition of color would enhance the work, you are encouraged to do what you must, though it is a good idea to test for color fastness before you incorporate it into the work. Once bound, it is difficult to undo without reducing your finished quilt to separate and myriad pieces. Avoid embroidery yarn, which has been known to ravel and fray.

Watch for breakage.

You must decide between two main types of sashing: *one-strip sashing* or *piece sashing*. Sashing is the interior border between each block; the border encompasses the entire work—in much the same way that the marriage vow encompasses your life together. One-strip sashing is fabric all of one piece, while pieced sashing allows for more than one fabric within the border. One-piece sashing is not for beginners. But, of course, you may be feeling particularly ambitious and lucky.

It is only in recent times that the bride has felt fortunate in marriage. Because she is encouraged to marry for love; not for family name or political alliance or wealth. No longer is she the unwilling spoil of war. The breathing tribute of a conquering tribe. No longer is she the stolen prize, crying for rescue, arms outstretched to her defeated kinsmen as she is spirited away. Yet, there are echoes of this theft today: the ritual bridal costume, the father relinquishing his daughter before the invited witnesses; the bride quietly leaving her own marital celebration while the guests continue to feast and dance. The cloister of the honeymoon, with its secret location that no one is privy to lest they track down and disturb the couple.

Many years ago, somewhere in Africa, the groom would prowl the bride's home, as if to kidnap her. Her response was to cry for help, to only pretend to resist. In other places she was exchanged for movable property.

Study the colors of the blocks. Do not be hasty when deciding on a border, as you will have to live with this choice the rest of your quilt's life. Some sashes and borders will be more complementary to the blocks than others. All sashing will divide, but some will enhance, bring out the best in the blocks, while others will dull the blocks, hide their original beauty. Marriage, too, can heighten the wife's colors or consign her to listless hues and shades.

Often, there is no way to know until you are joined. All you really have to go on is the faith of the kiss.

As you stitch the top cloth to the batting to the back work, baste all three layers together—for security and accuracy. Do not skimp on these steps. A little effort now will save you a great deal of effort later. You know that marriage and friendship require effort.

Pioneer quilts were bound, front to back, by knots with dangling strings.

The rose is bound to the earth by the dangle of its roots. Without roots, you are milkweed to the wind, drifting from place to place and never really arriving. On your bad days, this thought keeps you in bed longer than you should be in the mornings. On your good days, you revel in the lightness of wind-drifting because you understand that for a plant to survive its soil (a house to remain in good repair; a friendship to remain close), it must be carefully tended. Which adds up to a good deal of attention paid; attention you are sometimes not prepared to give.

Still, you are drawn to the bond of friendship, the marriage pact. Drawn and repelled, as if you do not know the difference (the benefits and hardships) between leaving and staying.

A bride carries a floral bouquet as she travels down the aisle. Castilian girls wear white flowers at their bosom; Andalusian girls with their hair alive with wreaths of small roses; the Hawaiian girl gently tucks a hibiscus behind one ear; the right means "spoken for," the left open to promises.

Your garden contains love-in-a-mist and honey-bear roses, which fill the air with an exceptionally sweet scent; only a few people are able to tolerate such a honey-sweetened atmosphere. And the climbing roses making their ascent toward sun and sky, bound at the root to the earth but longing for the sky.

Binding the quilt is not the same as laying the borders. Binding encompasses the entire work and may be achieved a couple of ways. You can turn the back edge forward. Be sure to leave a generous excess on the back work, enough to frame the top material. Or you can stitch on a separate edge. The separate edge is often recommended since it can be replaced if the quilt suffers from tension, stretching, age, or accident. Sometimes, a quilt can benefit from an attached border; can make the fusion whole yet relaxed.

The bride of one hundred years ago was often given a bridal friendship quilt on the day she was wed. Bringing something of value and use to the marriage, some little bit of personal property.

In America and England there were marriages known as "shift" or "closet" marriages, which protected a bride's property from her new husband's debtors. No one could show himself on the day after the wedding and say, with authority, to the newlyweds, *This is mine. This is what I am owed*. In the shift marriage the bride is systematically stripped to her undergarment as she approaches the altar, leaving her in a state of false poverty, as she stands, ashamed of her near nakedness, before her husband and minister. In the closet marriage, she is secreted in a closet with only her hand coming through a hole in the door to receive the ring.

The friendship quilt should have inked messages written upon its patches: wishing the woman well; good fortune for the newly married; quoting poetry or a wise saying or a bit of advice. Offering a warning or an admonition to be safe, to take care, and so long. Quoting scripture is common and not seen by the quilter as blasphemous.

Leaving or staying forces you to face the presence or absence of friends. The quilters will probably piece together a friendship quilt one day. It seems logical and correct. Historically it has its place for women who quilt. Peaking in popularity as American families pushed west, having already claimed the East, and friends said good-bye, certain not to meet again in this hard life. These journeys were uncertain, fraught with mystery. Manifest Destiny being all the rage in 1845.

You know, too, about pushing west and looking for fresh territory. You know about friendship and loss. Neruda has a second poem, written to his wife, regarding the earth but unlike the other earth poem, which relies on the sweetness of a kiss. This one says, *And each wound has the shape of your mouth.* But all you will remember when he is gone and you are almost friendless, is the mention of the kiss.

When you are making the friendship quilt you are declaring love and faithfulness in the face of parting, perhaps forever.

Say it with your hands.

Then wave good-bye.

String of Pearls

SOMETIMES, CONSTANCE SAUNDERS THINKS, THE worst thing about being a woman is having women friends. And the worst part about having women friends is that one must share so many confidences, except the one confidence Constance longs to share, which is the one about not being wild over the idea of women friends. Perhaps this life with Howell—this nomadic salesman drifting from town to city to town—has its moments of blessing. After all, if she is constantly being uprooted and moved, then she cannot truly make friends of any sort of depth, now can she?

It is not uncommon for Howell to sit across the table from her at supper, his eyes made slightly darker by his glasses, take her hand in his, and say, "I know this is a lonely life. All this moving makes it hard for you to have women friends. I never meant for you to not have any friends."

But Constance only smiles a closed-mouth smile, squeezes his hand in reply, then: "I know I have said this before, How, and you resist believing it to be true, but I *am* happy. That is, I am not lonely. I knew what our lives would be when I married you. When I fell in love with you." He looks her in the eye. "I'm fine," she says. "Trust me."

And she was fine. Constance long ago quit believing in lucky accidents and favored a more fatalistic turn of mind. You meet the man who will become your husband and his profession becomes your profession and maybe it is all for the best, in that respect. Her parents, of course, saw Howell Saunders as a timely lucky accident, since he married their Constance just shy of her thirty-third birthday. After all, she was the last child at home, unwed, and it seemed her prospects were getting slimmer and slimmer. Her two older brothers and three older sisters had all tried to introduce her around, "circulate" her socially, but to no avail—she simply did not seem to be interested. Her lack of interest appeared to extend to other women as well. Her parents worried that she was lonely.

What was strange about Constance was that she did not object to her single status; she accepted it in such a quiet way, it was puzzling. Sometimes her parents caught her gazing out the window or into the distance from the cool protection of the porch, indifferently sipping iced tea, and they were certain she was examining her solitary life. If only they had not been so old, they would not be as worried, but they could not live forever. They did not want to leave their baby alone in the world. They only hoped that when the time came, her siblings would allow her to remain in the family house.

The house was old and accommodating, set on

five acres in White Plains, New York, with trees and deer and that large, oddly shaped swimming pool, which was used exclusively by Constance. Perhaps it is a mistake to be "comfortable" and to have children who will grow up to be comfortable as well. Perhaps it kills the motivation.

Had her parents asked her, as she sat on the porch, looking off into the distance, Constance would have told them that she was considering a day trip into Manhattan, taking in a museum or two; maybe purchase something frivolous and useless to adorn her attractive throat.

At other times, she contemplated getting her own flat or small house; certainly she could afford it. She would swish the tea around in the tall glass. She might even get a roommate. Of course, it would have to be a woman, for form's sake, but that did not interest her. Suddenly, her dream house was transformed under the touch of this phantom female roommate; things were being made "nice" and there was supper together and emotional confessions and tales of personal histories—no, she simply was not patient enough for such close contact.

Better to live with a man; they are so straightforward; except he would probably expect her to care for the household—even though they would not be married, or even lovers—and this did not interest her either. Her parents did not raise her that way. Despite the recent protests for women's rights, despite the equal split in rent, she felt she would still be expected to cook and tidy up or supervise some other woman hired to cook and tidy up. No, that would not do. Women demanded your heart and men your body.

So her mother and father would see Constance slowly rise from her chair on the porch, pulling the hair back from her neck (stuck there by the summer heat and humidity), leaving her half-empty glass by the base of the lawn chair.

Then Howell appeared ("I met him in the city, actually, somewhere near the Frick," she told her parents) and courted her. And her days were passed with Howell, taking long drives and looking at country homes: pre-Revolutionary houses, converted barns, gatehouses; or city lofts; or two-story middle-class homes nestled in New Jersey; or the sad apartments of urban slum areas; or the elegant New York brownstones; or standing below tall apartment buildings, their heads tipped way back, as they tried to glimpse a penthouse or two.

When they had exhausted all available historic house and walking tours (occasionally repeating a particular favorite), they contacted realtors in various areas around Connecticut, Pennsylvania, New Jersey, and New York, pretending to be potential buyers just so they could get inside and feel a more intimate sense of the home.

It was not uncommon for them to buy street food from the numerous city vendors and wander around downtown, investigating older landmarks like the Algonquin or the Chelsea, as well as newer, architecturally known high-rises.

One night, as they stood in the cold, well-tended

garden of a late-nineteenth-century cottage in up-state New York, Howell said, "Marry me, Constance. We'll move someplace out west, someday buying a house of our own, and our neighbors will say, 'My God, they were living here before we moved here and that was twenty years ago and they looked ancient then.' We'll be one of those old couples that people admire without knowing them."

Constance resisted pointing out to him that one out of every three marriages was currently ending in divorce and that it was becoming increasingly less fashionable these days to marry at all, even for someone who was thirty-three (though she felt that many would still think that she was lucky to find someone who wanted her at all and that it would be stupid to let him "get away"). Despite her awareness of these modern social trends, here in the mid-sixties, she said "Yes" anyway.

He explained that he was going into sales and that "in the beginning I'll probably be on the road a lot—around Nevada, California, that sort of territory" and "do you think that you could live like that?"

Of course she could; Constance, who never minded solitude, and who was curious about California. Besides, it would eliminate all that roommate business.

Her parents were confused, pleased, and marginally upset. This was what they wanted for her, wasn't it? "Constance," they said, sitting on either side of her on the porch in late September, their sweaters buttoned up to their throats, "we are delighted that you are getting married . . . and yet . . . he's not . . . we hoped . . . frankly, we are wondering if maybe you aren't marrying beneath yourself."

Constance slouched back in her chair, swallowing a shot of brandy from a coffee mug. "I thought you'd be happy for me."

"We are," said her mother. "Naturally."

"I know," Constance said. "He's in sales." Constance got up and walked to the end of the porch before turning around and facing her aging parents. "I've been to college. I've been to Europe. I've spent weekends with the girls at Virginia Beach and out to the Island and up to the Cape and back to the shore. I'm not really fit for the workplace—surely you've noticed my lack of, ah, *ambition*—and I am almost thirty-three years old, and it occurs to me that if I don't marry Howell Saunders, I might be able to add old maid to that list of things that are me."

"Honey," said her mother in her Soothing Voice.

Constance shrugged her shoulders. "I'm not unhappy. Maybe being unhappy takes ambition, too." She rested her head against her hand on the pillar of the porch. "Mother, Dad, I think this is a good idea. I think it is what I need. Howell doesn't expect me to be something I so clearly am not."

"We certainly can't stop you." Her mother crossed her arms.

"No," said Constance, "you can't."

What Constance could not say to anyone was that she was beginning to feel like a freak of nature: She liked being alone; she was not excited about formal education, yet she loved to read and learn; nor was she desirous of being a traditional wife nor drawn to being a career woman. She was intrigued by the idea of romantic love. She wanted to feel safe. Constance wished she was exceptional in some way, but she was not. People are confused by women who are neither exceptional nor married; they seem to feel you should be one or the other.

The truly terrible thing in this life, she had long ago decided, was not knowing what you want, but only able to recognize what you do not want. You have to spend so much time and energy trying to figure it out, time that other people spend in pursuit of their desires.

The other freakish side of her nature was her impatience with other women. And to remain unmarried certainly seemed to sentence her to a life spent in the company of girlfriends, balanced by the occasional date. Oh, she was tired of explaining her unmarried state to family and friends, especially since she was not extraordinary or philosophically opposed to marriage.

It all boiled down to the same inescapable fact: that to live outside the mainstream one needed to be a rebel, and that she was not.

She was thirty-three, three short years from middle age, and a wealth of new aspects presented themselves: her parents' old age; the fact that her youth was really and truly gone from her and would not come again. Never again would she awaken in the morning, fresh and perfect by just tumbling out of bed; nor would young men regard her with promise. And she felt more mature inside as well.

She felt less frantic, calmer, yet terrified of other women and their talk of husbands and housework and help and hearth. (Terrified she might be making the wrong decisions.) And the subtle thickening of their thirtyish figures and their quiet, shrugging acceptance of all manner of things.

Of course, there were their counterparts: women of the same age who did not marry or married briefly at eighteen, only soon to divorce, and their cool mistrust of men; or their stale innocence, which invited disreputable men to use them over and over, each transgression forgiven as if it were an isolated incident.

Even the women who choose to remain unmarried and throw themselves entirely into their work seem to falter in the face of love.

Constance could not marry without affection. And there was Howell Saunders that day in the city, when she literally turned the corner and walked into him. They fell in love. Just like that. As Constance was gardening and planting freesia bulbs in the early winter, thinking how sort of wonderful he was; recall how he would spend time with her, listen to her and understand. She confessed her lack of ambition and direction and he nodded and listened. "He means it, too," she said aloud to herself, her bent knees crushing the lobelia that spilled out of its bed and onto the walkway. If she had to answer her parents' questions about why she loved Howell Saunders she would have to say: Because he lets me be.

Surely, she thinks, this must be the secret of marriage that no one seems inclined to recognize or practice. It was not an accident that Constance found herself drawn to Howell; it was an act of her nature.

He had not said a word about trying to change her. Not a word. They did not barter their future with words like "I'll do this if you'll do that" or "If you put up with this one thing for a while, I promise you things will be different in a few years." Howell told her: "Constance, I am moving to California. My job will take me on the road much of the time. As my wife you will be alone. I'd like to have children—but if we don't, I can live with that, too. If we do have children I can't promise that I'll be around more often. I hope one day it won't be that way, but I don't know. I promise I'll be faithful on the road but I can't promise that you won't be lonely."

She liked that. The forthrightness of it, as if he respected her too much to con her. He offered no guarantees except what he could guarantee—none of those silly promises about a future no one can foresee. He would do the best he could.

When she asks him questions about anything, he considers the answer and delivers it truthfully, not simply telling her what he thinks she wants to hear. Of all the things a man can do, she hates that falseness most of all: someone who tries to edit or predict her response before she makes it. To be second-guessed or "protected" from the truth is to be treated like a child.

The best men tell you the truth because they think you can take it; the worst men either try to preserve you in some innocent state with their false protection or are "brutally honest." When someone tells you the truth, lets you think for yourself, experience your own emotions, he is treating you as a true equal. As a friend.

And the best men cook for you.

Constance and Howell lived in a number of places for brief periods of time. Near Barstow, down to San Bernardino, Glendale, Visalia, a little past Lompoc, Buttonwillow, Los Banos—as far north as Crescent City, even into Medford, Oregon, for one dull two-month period. But never Nevada. And through it all Constance packed their few and functional belongings, since she could not tolerate the weight of so many material things, which only serve to slow your progress; sometimes she left things behind in some small bungalow or house or apartment in which they lived. Sometimes Howell traveled on ahead of her, searching for a new bungalow or small house or apartment. They saw the inside of so many homes, lived in so many different places, that their hunt occasionally recalled their courtship travels.

Since they did not live anyplace long enough to form deep friendships or attach themselves to any house or location, Constance felt no regret at moving on. Nor did she experience a profound searching inside herself, as if the next place would yield something better than the last; she simply packed up and moved, and was often glad to do so.

During these years Constance forgot how to say good-bye or bid farewell since she rarely left anyone or anything of any significance. This suited her: all that temporary living combined with periods of solitude. Her parents wanted to know if she was happy. ("Yes, I am happy.") Did she need money? Want a permanent home of her own? And her reply was always "I have what I need. I lack for nothing."

And Howell and Constance grew closer during his time spent home between trips, being each other's only friend. *Funny,* thinks Constance, *that I should so like being married. I never expected to like it this much.*

Howell returned from a business trip and said, "Constance, I miss you." Then told her how he found a small house in Atwater with French doors and roses outside the window. (Years later Constance will say to the women in the quilting circle, "The garden was a mess—overgrown, dried-out, unpruned, in places overwatered by someone who did not understand the lives of roses—but it was a real rose garden. And we had a dog, a peach-colored poodle mix named Chickie. Our Chickie was the best dog—not one of those spoiled yappers that can drive a person crazy.")

And so began a life where Howell left and returned each day like a regular husband, kissing Constance at the door, dropping on all fours to play with Chickie. Children were not a consideration for them—now, of course, it was simply too late—but even in the beginning they each thought that, at thirty-three, Constance was truly past her childbearing years. Or perhaps it was something else; an excuse. Regardless, she did not conceive.

The children of the neighborhood adopted Constance and Howell, often bringing treats to Chickie. Constance greeted the children by saying, "Well, *hello*, and how are you? Have you grown since you were last here? No? Maybe you only *seem* bigger because you act so grown up." The children would clamor for Chickie, who raced out to see them. Sometimes they brought Chickie bones; if they brought the "wrong" kind of bones (the sort that splinter), Constance put them in her pocket, promising to give them to Chickie later, after dinner, "for dessert."

When Chickie died—an early dog death, actually—Howell and Constance buried her in the rose garden beneath an antique yellow rosebush. After that, yellow roses were always referred to as "Chickie's flowers."

(Constance will tell Marianna, years later, as they are gardening in Glady Joe's yard, "After Chickie's death it was so hard to leave that little house. Every place changes when you bury someone you love there. That is how it was for me, after Chickie.")

Howell quit his stationary Atwater job and hit the road again. They moved and resided in a succession of apartments, trailers, and two-bedroom homes that sat behind larger, nicer homes. Constance missed her prize roses, left in Atwater with her most beautiful bush sheltering Chickie's grave. Sometimes they lived someplace long enough for her to plant and care for a garden, but that was rare. Then, one day, Howell said, "No more, Constance—life's too short and I've had enough.

Baby, I'm home for good." Constance was sitting at the kitchen table in the late-morning sun when Howell came to the door, stood within its frame, and said, Baby, I'm home for good.

At first, she looked up from her book but said nothing, did nothing; after all, she had already kissed him good-bye this morning when he had gone to work, and seeing him standing there, unexpectedly, made her wonder if she was only imagining his ghost, that if she so desired she could stand and walk right through his outline.

Then she laid the book down (carelessly closing it without marking her place) and pushed her chair from the table, and with slow, deliberate steps, walked in his direction, sliding her arms around his waist, resting her cheek against his coat.

He held her so tightly it was hard to fill her lungs with air, and thinking back on that moment, she could've sworn she felt his chest heave in a small sob.

Constance and Howell got on each other's nerves. His being retired and always around caused Constance to blurt out, "Don't you have somewhere to go?" And he looked at her, saying, "Don't *you*?" There were days when she felt hemmed in, crowded in her own house, as if Howell were not one person but a small group that made continuous, inconsequential demands of her time and patience, which, taken together, resulted in an enormous demand that she could never satisfy. She tried to explain this to him, but he only looked at her and said, "What exactly are you saying?"

"I don't know what I'm saying," she answered in an irritated tone of voice. "I mean, I feel like . . ."

Howell looked at her patiently, as if trying to divine her true desires. "Do you want me to leave?"

"Oh, no," she said. "No. I want you to, well, go out sometimes. Without me. More often than you do." How could she say, You've made me grow accustomed to a life without you around all the time. Seeing you occasionally seemed less like a marriage and more like an extended courtship or love affair, with the time spent together so rich and brief that we could not spend it arguing or in silent discord. Instead we chose to use the time with our best courtship personas: lying in the garden in the dirt and grass, staining and muddying our clothes but not caring; watching the clouds or talking about your travels or my books or what so-and-so is up to or rehashing the time we met and fell in love; or cooking and taking our meals to bed, feeding each other and laughing about the way some couples Simply Despise It when the other spouse eats off their plate, as you licked spilt cake crumbs from my body.

A next-door neighbor once said to Constance after she said good-bye to Howell before one of his road trips, "How long have you two been married?"

When Constance said, "Fifteen years," the neighbor replied, "You'd never know it from the way you two act."

"How's that?" asked Constance.

"You act as if you like each other."

Constance started to say, That's awfully cynical,

don't you think? but the neighbor headed her off, as she turned to walk back to her house, by saying, "I meant *exactly* what I said."

But now that Howell was retired, Constance yearned for the vast, empty hours that had stretched before her when he was away on business, the sheer pleasure of anticipating his return. Even in Atwater, he worked eight hours a day, which was enough solitude for her. But this constant state of togetherness was wearing on her. What did this say about the nature of their marriage? About her nature? That she was not cut out to be a wife, only to be a girlfriend? After all, Howell did not seem to be experiencing the deep irritation at her daily company that she felt for his.

Then, just as suddenly, the feeling fled. Inexplicably, strangely, quickly—it just left her; and for the first time in her life she thought, *How truly happy I am!* She marveled at the feeling, luxuriated in it, wondered how she could have thought she was happy all those previous years, then decided that she had not been profoundly happy, only content. It was as if something inside herself gave way, softened, relaxed its hold. She gave in to the luxury of having him around always and basked in his company. Now she felt just the smallest bit of sadness when he ran errands or took drives without her.

The one night a week she spent quilting at Glady Joe Cleary's house became a chore. She had become friendly with Marianna Neale, as they shared an affection for roses; was grateful to have her in the quilting circle with her. (She still had not grown used to groups of women and felt an undefined restlessness around them, making her appreciative of Marianna, with whom she felt a comfortable kinship.) This was in Grasse, where Howell said to her, *Baby, I'm home for good.*

She did not especially enjoy quilting or sewing, brought little imagination to the work, but the repetition functioned as therapy, giving focus to her disjointed and unpeopled life. When she discovered the impulsive, unplanned *Crazy Quilt*, she became more interested and adept at the work. As far as patterns went, her favorite was called *My Grandmother's Flowers*, which she modified, using only yellow roses, and renamed *Chickie's Garden*.

Now she had this new feeling regarding her marriage. *Perhaps I had to keep a locked restraint on my affection for Howell, knowing he would always come and go and never stay for good. Is this how I would've felt had we always been together?* She thought about their life in Atwater, realizing for the first time that, yes, those were the happiest years before these and that she refused to see it at the time (refused to surrender to her own happiness), knowing he could again change jobs. But then, if they had spent all those years together in a conventional marriage, maybe they would've become like her cynical neighbor—a couple who loved each other but did not like each other—as if love is some sort of virus and marriage the agent that makes one immune to the illness by overexposure. Imagine being immune to married love.

But one day, as Howell was getting his hair cut, he quietly slumped in the barber's chair, and

Constance did not cry or have a memorial service. Em Reed and Anna Neale thought she showed disrespect to Howell's memory, but Constance rarely explained herself to anyone and certainly not to this group of women she quilted with, women who rushed sympathetically to her side, while Constance only wished to be left alone.

Constance ordered a plain pine box, allowed a rabbi to say a prayer as she rent a small piece of her clothing, this nod to her husband's long-neglected religious beliefs, beliefs she did not share. Then she had Howell quietly buried.

(When someone dies, the funeral is the measure of his life. How many mourners will there be? Will they arrive on time? Will they come to the house later? Bring food? Or, will there be any mourners at all? Howell, with all his traveling, worked alone; all the moving around did not lend itself to long-term friendship. She would not hold a funeral for this wonderful man who had been her husband, with only a few people in attendance. She did not care for herself, but she did not want him to know how lonely an empty chapel can be.)

She went alone to his grave (no tears), her arms loaded down with roses: peach, yellow, pink, apricot, salmon, and pale orange. She laid them across the freshly turned earth.

Afterward, as she sat in the booth of a coffee shop, she heard a man ask, "May I sit with you?" It was Dean Reed, Em's husband. "Jesus," he said, sliding across from her, "I'm sorry about Howell."

Constance drank her coffee and thanked him.

"Are you all right?" he asked. "Is there anything I can do?"

Constance smiled. "You can take me dancing."

Dean looked horrified.

"I'm sorry," she said, pushing her saucer away from her slightly. "Howell was a good man and I loved him. But he's gone now." She paused. "I don't believe in grief."

"How can you not 'believe in grief'?" Dean asked. "Either you grieve or you don't."

Constance shrugged her shoulders, snapped open her handbag, and paid the check. It was getting dark outside. Dean offered to drive her home, but she told him, "I feel like walking."

"Look," he said, standing beside her on the sidewalk outside, "I know how things can be around the house. Give me a call if you ever need anything, like painting or the plumbing fixed."

Constance put on her sunglasses (though it was dusk). "Thanks—I'll keep that in mind." It had not occurred to her until this moment that she might move somewhere else, another state or country. Without Howell, she really did not belong anywhere. But as she headed home, her pace picked up as the tears began creeping down below her sunglasses, she realized that this place, with its quilters and hot summers and Dean and her friendship with Marianna (the first real woman friend she ever had, who gardened by her side or she by Marianna's side), had now changed for her. Now, with Howell buried here, it had become someplace else, someplace she could not leave.

* * *

Dean began dropping by Constance's to see if she "needed anything." Often she did not, though occasionally there would be something that required attention; something to be moved or tightened or discarded or stowed. More often, Dean simply sat with Constance and reminisced about the East Coast, having been born and raised in Morristown, New Jersey.

He relaxed on her sofa or in the surreal disappearing light of the autumn afternoon (the time of day professional photographers call "magic hour" for its sensationally flattering light), and said, "Of course, when it was springtime I would say that was my favorite season; in the fall I would say, 'No, this is the best time of year.' I have an affection for those transitional seasons, the way they take the edge off the intense cold of winter or heat of summer. But I often think that spring and autumn would completely lose their charm without those extremes of weather in winter and summer."

"I know," Constance agreed, "but I have to say spring is my favorite, with dogwood, foxglove, columbine, corn salad, Victoria blues coming up and my roses. Daffodils, fuchsia, and honeysuckle. What could be better?"

"Which brings me to this god-awful place virtually without seasons." He leaned forward on the couch, pushing his glass toward Constance across the coffee table, indicating that it needed "freshening." "How do these Californians stand it? It makes one lazy as hell. With so much of the year like summer, who rushes out to do any sort of summertime things? I mean, what is the hurry—the sun will be back tomorrow. And the next day and the next."

Constance poured out martinis for each of them, Howell's enormous watch sliding down her wrist as she held back the ice with her two fingers ("I'll bring you a strainer for the next time I come," he said). "I don't know. It would almost seem that a life without seasons would make you tense, as if you need the change of weather just to ease the pressure." She took a sip of her drink. "But I suppose you don't miss what you never had."

She sat back in her chair. Constance knew she should switch on the lights; soon it would be too dark to make out Dean's face, which was already fading in the shadows. Except that she liked the shadows, and since Howell's death she had had to sleep with a light or two on, which denied her the pleasure of sleeping in a blackened room. As a child she'd liked sleeping in the dark, and as an adult slept fitfully if too much light leaked in; even a particularly bright moon kept her in a state of half slumber, half wakefulness. When Howell was away she would sit up long into the night, engrossed in a project or a book, still rising at daybreak, when the house filled with sunlight. And for the rest of the day she would drag around in a stupor of fatigue because she was incapable of sleeping late or taking a nap.

When Howell was alive and traveling, she could still remain in the dark and take pleasure in it; perhaps because she knew that he would be returning to her. But all she had left to her now was his watch and his pajama tops, which she wore at night, his rose gold cuff links, transformed into earrings (a gold so soft and pale it looked as if it would take the image of a fingerprint if pinched with the slightest pressure), his great coat warming her in the garden on cold days, hitting her mid-calf where it had once grazed Howell's knees. Wearing his things as if she could absorb him, truly blur the line between her life and his death, intersect the planes of existence. She shook her head, causing Dean to interrupt himself and ask, "What?"

"Nothing," she said, embarrassed, bringing her drink to her lips, as he went on saying, "It's more than seasonal with these people in Grasse—there is something so, so, *monochromatic* about who they are as well. As if the weather goes deeper into who they are."

Constance smiled in the darkness; listened to Dean ramble on and on about the citizens of Grasse and their shortcomings. "Gee, I didn't realize how late it was," he said as Constance enjoyed these moments of darkness, felt secure and happy and relieved, as if some enormous weight had been lifted. Something she could not indulge in when alone in the house, now with Howell really and truly gone from her.

"I miss home sometimes," said Dean. "It's different out here—maybe I'm too hard on the place, but it isn't my landscape, if you know what I mean. Em and I only moved here to please her. I was so cynical I thought all places would be the same to me; I thought it was a weakness to love something as much as I loved the greenery of home. All that lawn. All that lush foliage."

"Sometimes I wake up at night and think to

myself, 'Now exactly how did I get here?' But I know I won't leave," said Constance.

"How do you know that?"

"I just do."

"Why not?" asked Dean, shifting forward, stirring his olive around in his glass. "I mean, why not just go?" Then softer, "Why don't I just go?"

Constance reluctantly turned on a lamp, felt sadness as the night was forced from the room. "Because we can't. Because we have things that keep us here now."

"But why should that be?" insisted Dean. "We're not dead yet."

"Oh, Dean," said Constance, "only someone very young can do that—move without hesitation—because the older you are, whether you intend it or not, you get attached. You lay down roots, feel an uncomfortable kinship with the soil beneath your feet. Certain things become meaningful and irreplaceable and no matter how much you like to travel or adore your destinations, you will always return to that thing that only exists for you here." She drained her glass. "And that, Dean, is the only difference I can see between youth and old age. Really. When you get down to it. I mean, nothing else changes, not the capacity to love or experience sexual jealousy or desire; or ambition in business or to be athletic or create art or parent a child—all that remains intact, despite our outer selves. It is the difference between digging in or moving on." She laughed nervously. Said, "Listen to me."

"Did you like the snow?" he asked.

"Very much so."

"Difficult weather, those gray-and-white winters. Hard on the body. Good way not to brood, I think."

Everyone is aware that Dean is stopping by Constance's house in the evenings, and this causes discomfort and dissension among the quilters; especially since Constance is a bit younger than the rest of them (certainly younger than Em). Closer to Marianna's age, mid-fifties. And Constance is an outsider as well. No one in the circle had grown up with her; shared her secrets.

Finn notices that some of the women side with Em, but one or two are noncommittal on the matter. They seem to believe that Constance and Dean are "just friends"; still, all this tension remains vague and free-floating, as if no one will allow it to find its proper focus.

It is Marianna who comes to Constance's rescue, defends her to the other women, including her mother, Anna, who says, "I only know what I see because I've seen it before." It is Marianna who sets free the collective rumor that lodges doubt in their collective judgment. She says, Look, nothing is going on. The quilters pay attention because Marianna is the closest thing Constance Saunders has to a friend, unless you count Dean, and there are clear problems in that regard. Of course.

Constance says, "Marianna, don't you get lonely?" as she prunes back a rosebush. As she and Marianna work in her garden.

"Didn't you get lonely when Howell was gone so

much?" Marianna asks, her hands moving gracefully from stem to stalk, encased in their bulky gardening gloves. ("Clown's hands," she calls them.)

"No," says Constance. "Which I don't exactly understand unless I was lonely all those years and didn't know it. Maybe I was always isolated—my whole life—until Howell came home for good." She leans back on her heels, her own clownish hands resting on her thighs. "Do you suppose that's possible? To feel something so essentially human and not know it at all?" Constance shakes her head. "I just never thought that I made very good company."

Marianna concentrates on her task, her mouth curving up at the corners, but she does not take her eyes from her work. "I know what you mean," she says.

But as to the question of loneliness or willful isolation or the difficulty in connecting properly with other people, Marianna wants to say: Try being black in Grasse—or Bakersfield, for that matter—growing up with your mother a housekeeper and your father—well, he never knew you. Then make the mistake of getting a college degree—before civil rights—and then you are really persona non grata around these parts so you have to run so far away to another country because you are a stranger in your own land. And because you remain outside any sort of mainstream life you become an anomaly, frightening even to yourself, when you discover that you can only relate to men and not to women because women demand too much talk, too much conversation, and confidences from you and you've reached the point in your life (oh, too long ago to remember) where you are too angry for "polite" conversation; you don't want to nurture or have your hand held in sympathy; why, you even surprise yourself with wanting to rip the world from its axis. You want to stop it from rotating one more frustrating day. And you suppose all this makes you not quite a woman and certainly not a man, but a complete outsider. And there you are.

Marianna has lived such a private, interior life that, as much as she likes Constance, she still cannot reveal herself. It is not her way, and she senses that Constance is the only woman in the quilting circle who would understand that because Constance is like her in that respect.

"What I like about you, Marianna," says Constance, "is that you remind me of Howell. You let me be." She stops and stares at Marianna. "Why is it that you don't ask me about Dean?"

Marianna sighs and turns toward her friend. "Now, don't take this wrong, Constance, but I guess I just don't care." She rubs the tip of her nose with her bulky glove. "God, I know that sounds terrible."

Constance considers this and says, "No. It is what I expected." She pats the earth firmly around the base of an iris stalk. "Look," she says, "I miss Howell, but you and Dean are the reasons I am not completely lonely." She places her hand over her heart, without awareness, leaving smudges of dirt on her shirt. Lightly thumps her chest, once, twice: "Most of the time, anyway."

* * *

However, there came a night when Constance and Dean walked out to his car—Howell had been gone close to a year—and Dean got behind the wheel only to turn on the ignition and hear (along with the rev of the engine) the radio playing "String of Pearls." Constance took a few steps from the car door as Dean, without a word, got back out and took her in his arms, pressing her close as they danced in the road. The car's headlights stared out ahead of them, illuminating the empty road. There was nothing before them. She sighed as she recalled their coffee-shop conversation the day of Howell's funeral.

Dean's unshaven cheek felt harsh against her skin; her body welcomed his touch and for the first time, after all these months, she saw Dean as a man and not as Em's husband. Though they did not sleep together, Constance dropped from the quilting circle for a while and kept to herself.

Instructions No. 4

A POPULAR QUILT OF THE 1920s WAS THE APPLIQUÉ quilt. It is still well thought of and considered a "better quality" quilt among collectors. It was usually favored by a higher economic stratum of women, since one had to be able to afford yards of the same cloth to achieve the proper effect. As opposed to the piece quilt, which was typified by its use of leftover scraps. No one, least of all yourself, really likes anything left over, something that, by its very nature, is shared with someone else. You feel this way about food, antique-clothing stores (used shoes give you a particularly creepy, unwholesome feeling, but then, you are a child of the 1930s), old houses, used cars, and gentlemen on the rebound. You desire your own, brand-new, unused whatever it is; you want it to be exclusively yours, bear your mark.

You may want to display what is yours, revel in your association with something of value. There are a number of ways to display a quilt upon a wall. One is to sew Velcro along the top edge, in the back, taking care not to pierce the front of the work. Then attach an equal length of Velcro to the wall, using a staple gun. Consider stitching a small square of Velcro to each corner to prevent buckling. Allowing for smoothness.

Or pretend you are stretching canvas to frame. Build the frame. You have seen this done in your own home, by your own husband; you are no stranger to art or display or the blank canvas. Be extravagant and install small hinges in each corner, in order to fold up the frame should you grow tired of displaying the quilt or should the man you adore grow tired of you, leaving you in need of a new residence; or find another use for the quilt other than display; or simply grow tired of looking at the work of the artist. Apply Velcro to the edge of the frame; likewise to the quilt. Take the exact measurements of the quilt. Remember, measure twice, cut once. Tear the quilt from the frame—as you have been afraid that you will be torn from the fabric of your marriage—for convenient cleaning or storage.

Bear in mind that storing a quilt may protect it from the elements of heat and dampness and light, but it will not afford anyone, including yourself, any pleasure in its beauty. This is sometimes forgotten by the avid collector who seeks to own but not to enjoy. Can you relax if your husband is not in clear sight? Does it make you anxious to wonder what he is doing without you? Away from you. Picture him flirting with a random girl in town (someone you have not noticed) whom he has found worthy of his attention—no matter how momentarily. Wish for an instant that you could place him somewhere and only take him out for your private viewing pleasure, that he would be grateful for your admiration. Allow yourself to enjoy your quilt.

The display method most popular with galleries and museums involves a ten-inch piece of muslin, hidden quilt threads, staples, and a wood frame. You could easily discover the more exact way of doing this. It is not an obscure method. Part of your problem is that you discover so many things with great ease and that is often more a curse than a blessing; clearly there are things you'd rather not know. But to hang a quilt this way may be more work than you wish to do.

Finally, and this is recommended only for the serious, experienced framer, one who is interested in making both a sizable financial investment, as well as one of time and skill: Buy a large, "quilt-size" piece of Plexiglas. Leave the back open for the work to "breathe." Nothing, you know, can be kept inviolate, in a box, away from the harm that can be inflicted on a marriage by a wandering husband who has so often told you that he cannot help but wander. He wishes it was not so because he loves you; because, he says, you are his lifeline; because it distresses him to the depths of his spirit to make you cry, to make you suffer. Out in the world, he cannot be trusted.

Find this sort of quilt preservation a relief when your friends who smoke or who are careless (a careless couple can murder love if left unchecked) come to your house for supper and stop to admire your beautiful quilt. (You like that, their admiration for something you have; yet you cannot help but worry that it will be appropriated by one of them.)

Remind yourself that they are your friends and can be trusted. Remind yourself that sometimes accidents happen and it will break your heart to see your quilt damaged.

It means that much to you.

You would sometimes rather it did not.

Drawbacks of this method—quilt in Plexiglas box—include losing a sense of intimacy with the work. The desire to touch the quilt will be harbored within yourself as well as within your guests—and perhaps the girl in town whom he flirted with—but they will simply have to imagine the feel of the small stitches, softness of the material, unevenness of the texture (all of which gives your quilt its look of life), the extra puff of stuffing in selected areas of the top cloth, not to be confused with the layer of cotton batting that lies between the backing and the top work. Do not neglect to note that this sort of display treatment renders the quilt more formidable as a work of art. An ordinary, useful household item transformed. Shake your head at such a transformation.

A tint on the Plexiglas will afford more protection from the light that enters the room, visits itself upon the quilt. Protects it from fading. You could find yourself overwhelmed by all the precautions necessary to protect your quilt, all the machinations to keep it in good condition. The women of your circle agree that it is worth it; anything worth having is worth guarding against losing. Your marriage is worth guarding; you are told passion fades. But, again, the trade-off is that it gives your quilt a textureless, lifeless appearance. You may not want to surrender it to this fate.

You may be willing to risk it. You did not marry to police another human being. You misguidedly thought that love would sustain you both; that it would be enough. That the threads comprising the fabric of your marriage would not break for any reason; that they would be stronger for their closeness and proximity to one another. You make the sad discovery that, though you and he are joined as one, you are not the same person; that marriage can require more than love. It shocks your sensibilities, this idea that love is not the greatest force in life. Or perhaps it does not mean the same thing to everyone.

About the light in the room: It can and will fade your quilt. Perhaps you like the way it looks when the early-morning sun lies across it, lazylike, taking its sweet morning time, warms the room, brings out the colors; but be warned that this will ultimately damage the quilt.

Your choices are clear: Place a shade in the window or move the quilt. There really is no gray area; one or the other. Anything else places the quilt at risk. Fading is to be avoided because it leaves the quilt in a tainted condition, allowing you only the memory of what it once was. Trust yourself. There is no in-between.

Umbrellas Will Not
Help at All

SUCH A CORROSIVE RAIN AS ON VENUS WOULD be one of the most potent and destructive fluids in the solar system. It would burn away human flesh in a matter of minutes. Umbrellas would not help at all.

Em Reed is not looking forward to stitching the next project, a *Crazy Quilt*. She knows the responsibility of the quilter is different in this sort of quilt. She knows, too, that while her contribution will appear to be random, it will, in fact, be freighted with personal meaning. (She has heard talk that they may assemble a bridal quilt for Finn Bennett-Dodd and Em does not know if she has the patience to put herself into a work that holds marriage as its center.) The other quilters will ask privately or speculate about her patches, and Em is not imaginative enough to lie. So she is miserable.

Not like Dean can lie, she thinks. For the past eight months he has been making regular, open visits to Constance Saunders, ever since Howell passed on. Em thinks widows should accept their solitude with grace and not attempt to replace the man they lost with another woman's husband.

The worst of it, of course, is having to sit in the same room, quilting with Constance, Howell's reading glasses large on her small face, sliding down her nose as she bends over the work. Watching her clumsy hands push the needle through the fabric, making Em wonder if her own hands look as graceless. Thinking Dean may even find Constance's hands elegant; he used to find Em's hands elegant, and Em knows what love can do to Dean. Everything is filtered through his painter's eye and faithless heart. Sometimes Constance whispers to Marianna, and though Em cannot make out what she is saying, she is pierced through the heart by the softness of her voice.

Anna Neale told her that it doesn't matter, that as long as Dean keeps coming home at night that's all Em needs to know. Em wants to say, Anna, you don't know what you are talking about, since Anna never married, but refrains. She even stops herself from kicking Constance's chair when she passes behind her or jabbing her with a sharp needle or screaming at her to find her own man. She may need the sympathy of the other quilters, if it comes down to it; but there is another reason, and it is that it would not change a thing in Em's life.

What Em cannot bring herself to tell the other quilters is that this is not Dean's first affair; the first one occurred in the early years of their marriage. It isn't even his second affair. Dean wanted to be a painter (he was actually quite gifted) but his dream somehow failed him, leaving him to teach art to students with less skill and vision. He was frustrated, as creative people denied their outlet often are. He grew moody, restless, cruel within his own home, blaming everyone for his failure; blaming himself, too. Other days he would be buoyed by a sense of hope, happy and affectionate.

Still, three years into their marriage, Em considered divorcing Dean over that first affair. Dean was not what the circle would call a "decent man," because of his changeable moods and thwarted talent; his unpredictable, cynical nature excluded him from the company of decent men. But no one knew that he was unfaithful to Em.

Em can still hear herself saying to Sophia Richards, "Don't be ridiculous—she is his student and nothing more. Surely he is allowed to take on private students?" Or, again to Sophia, "Christ, I can't believe how people in this town talk and talk and know absolutely nothing about anything."

Sophia said, "Em, I'm your friend." Her elbow was propped on the table, her chin set on the back of her hand. Sophia seemed to look past Em with a gentle, unfocused gaze. "I know husbands," she added. "I know Dean."

This caught Em by surprise, caused her to wonder what Sophia meant by 'I know Dean,' then shook her head. Sophia understood nothing about her marriage. "No, not this time," said Em.

Sophia shrugged her shoulders as Em resisted the temptation to confide in her best friend. She could not tolerate being placed in the position of confessing Dean's betrayal and defending him at the same time.

Because Em hated the idea of marriages based on suspicion and mistrust, she virtually refused to believe Dean's betrayal at first. She knew he was unlike the farmers, ranchers, and small businessmen who comprised the region; she married him for his lack of convention. Now she wanted him to behave like a "normal" husband. Em used to say to herself, *It is not within me to be "different," though I long for it.* So, as with poor or socially unconnected women who marry for money or prestige, Em married a man who rough-handed convention because she was not brave enough to do it for herself.

Clearly, she saw marriage as a joining of complements to create a whole.

Em wanted to stick with Dean (after that first girl), not consider divorce, because she understood his anger and his unused gift; she eventually forgave him, because she understood him, but she was no longer sure that she liked or respected him. Oh, she still loved him, but he did not feel like a friend to her any longer. She can recall sitting in a bath when the water had turned lukewarm, the bubbles deflated and all but dirty little edges of foam clinging to the tub corners. She remembers being half turned toward Dean, who crouched beside her on the bathroom rug (his large feet leaving indentations in the pile), her wrinkled, waterlogged fingers gripping the edge of the tub as she tried to puzzle out his affection for the other girl. "But," she asked, confused, "is it something I am not doing? Is it me?" And then, as if she were commenting on someone else's life instead of her own, "To think we love each other."

It occurred to her that perhaps she did not respect herself. Is it possible to cleave to a man before the eyes of God, become one with him, be unable to respect him, yet retain self-respect? Particularly if you view marriage as combined halves that make a whole? She did not know; they were already too much a part of each other to know.

And, later, when she stood in their bedroom in her robe, Em broached the idea of divorce, prompting Dean to weep freely in her arms, telling her to do what she had to do, begged her not to go, admitted that he was hard to live with but loved her just the same.

In her heart, Em mistakenly thought that this man was meant to be her burden, the experience to strengthen her, make her so powerful nothing could touch her.

A year later she discovered that Dean had a new woman. All Em knew was that she was two years older than Dean and had something to do with the college that employed him. Em sobbed and asked, "How could you do this to me again? Why do you keep doing this?" Deep inside she wondered with a sort of detached curiosity if perhaps she was unlovable or if there were strict time limits to the length of loving her and maybe three or four years was its duration. "Why are you doing this?"

Dean was quiet, his voice low and defeated. "I do love you," he told her.

Em's tears washed the heels of her hands, the backs of her slim fingers.

"Em," he said, "I am a man out of control. I can't be a painter; I can't improve my lot and I can't live with it. I'm cynical and hard and cursed to see the world in romantic terms."

Em looked at him with furious, wet eyes. She thought him a remarkably selfish sonofabitch. She said, "You bastard."

And she thought of something else: When only a year before he had ended the first affair, the girl called the house, once or twice, crying for Dean. "If I could just talk to him for a minute," she said, "I could get some sleep tonight and never bother you again. I promise." But Em would have none of her promises and only turned the phone over to Dean, whose face took on a harsh, irritated expression when he said, taking a deep breath, "What do you want from me? I have already said all there is to say." Then his voice yielded just slightly (with an imperceptibility only a wife could detect) and he said, "I know. I know. Didn't I tell you this was not good. Couldn't you tell?"

Em had crossed her arms and pulled her mouth into a tense line, causing Dean to turn his back on her and cut the conversation short. But Em could've sworn she heard him whisper *baby* into the phone just before he said he was sorry, he really was, but it was over and she would have to accept it. Down the receiver came into the cradle and Dean wandered from the room, but not before he stopped and gently touched Em's bare arm. She heard him in his studio, stapling stretched canvas to a wooden frame, and then silence; a brush stroke is like a whisper in a cave and cannot be heard unless you are in close proximity.

At that time, Em would bang up to their bedroom or take long, angry walks, her steps violent, often mumbling to herself; reminding herself that he showed remorse and good faith, that he promised not to do it again, and that everyone makes a mistake and where would we all be if we didn't express a little forgiveness now and then? And at other moments, even worse, for no reason, Em would feel herself in a fury—sometimes in the middle of a perfectly good dinner or day outing or dance—where she would be inexplicably happy in Dean's presence, loving him, and like a sudden fever her anger would well to the surface, blacken her mood, and cause him to pull away, contrite. She would turn to him, regardless of where they were or what they were doing, and say, "I want to go home. *Now.*"

There was the day when they drove down to Los Angeles to see an exhibit at the Museum of Art and she hauled off and clipped him, closed-fisted, in the jaw, when only a moment before she had snuggled beneath his arm.

"What the hell is it with you?" he demanded, holding down her arm, his grip tight, looking, Em thought, as if he wanted to strike her in return.

"I never should have allowed you to be forgiven. I should have forced you to leave."

"Is that what you want?"

"What I *want*," she said in measured tones, "is for you and that girl to never have happened. What I *want* is to punish you. I don't feel as if you have suffered."

"Very nice, Em."

"I want to hurt you."

And then it would all pass and she would apologize and he would apologize and they would renew their promise to love and take care of each other, Em convinced that one recovers from these things as one does an illness.

Now it was happening all over again and he was telling her, "The only thing I can change or control—the only adventure I can find," he said, "is love."

Em flew at his face, beating him about the head with a vicious fury. Pantings and yelps escaped her throat as she attacked him. He had taken advantage of her understanding nature. Dean did not fight her off but shielded himself. Em had tried to give him what he needed—understanding, forgiveness. Having satisfied those needs, he created more needs and turned to someone new for satisfaction. His personal needs were greater than her understanding, greater than the sum of their marriage.

Em walked out. She went to her mother's house. She was thankful that they did not have any children.

At her mother's house she discovered that she was pregnant.

And still she did not go back.

Dean called her at Christmas. He said, "Merry Christmas, Em," and she hung up on him without a word because she knew that he had nothing but contempt for the holidays, for the "poor fools" who thought these things mattered and don't get him started on the absence of true religion in the month of December. She was eight weeks pregnant and laid low by morning sickness and a sort of general malaise. Her mother said, "When I was first pregnant with you all I ever did was eat and sleep and wish for it to be over."

"Did it get better?" asked Em from the sofa, where she lay with closed eyes, in a half-dream state that included a curiously welcome hallucination of Dean.

Her mother held out an unwrapped chocolate kiss to her daughter, who parted her lips, allowing her mother to place it in her mouth.

"Well," her mother said, smiling, "yes and no. That is, the second trimester was the best, but the other times, honey, you'll have to decide for yourself."

"Thanks for the encouragement."

"Sweetie, if you want a fairy story, ask your doctor about pregnancy. I'm sure he'll tell you whatever you want to hear."

"Will I ever stop being so tired?" Em felt as if her voice were floating, circling around her there on the couch. She wished her mother would catch it, nail it down.

"Sure, sweetie." She patted her daughter's leg, as Em drifted off into a nap.

HAPPY NEW YEAR said the telegram, signed LOVE-STOPDEAN, which Em tore up and dropped in the garbage. There was a delivery of irises and King

Alfred daffodils with a hand-painted box of choco-
lates for St. Valentine's Day. Birthday greetings came
in April, followed by a big basket of lilies, marsh-
mallow chicks, and an alabaster egg for Easter. All
of which ended up in the trash. All of which arrived by messenger and not delivered by Dean. "At
least he knows not to show up himself," said Em.

Sophia Richards stopped by occasionally, pregnant by this time with her second child, often with
serious little Duff in tow. She had begun quilting
over at Glady Joe Cleary's house and insisted that
Em join them. At first, Em said no, she rather liked
being at her parents' house and not having to travel
through Grasse, where she might catch a glimpse of
Dean, with god knows who on his arm. She liked
being here, away from Grasse, with no thought of
anything. Only her mother's soothing company or
watching her father in his workshop.

One evening, at dusk, during that very hot
spring, Em, seven months pregnant, sat on the
porch of her parents' house. She had just emerged
from the small wading pool her father built when
she was a child. Her belly was straining against the
fabric of an old slip of her mother's. As she sat on
the porch, wringing water from the hem of the wet
slip, running her fingers through her short hair, and
shaking herself free of the water, Dean drove up.
She froze and gripped the arms of the metal chair
she was sitting in; her body pulled slightly forward,
as though involuntarily drawn to him. Em did
not rise as he approached (she was a very clumsy

woman in her seventh month and could no longer trust her sense of balance).

"Hey, Em," said Dean, standing before her.

"Hi," said Em, smiling.

Dean leaned toward her, fingering her wet hair. Then he fell to his knees, placed his body between her parted legs, running his hands around her wide hips. His cheek resting on her tight belly.

Em's hands did not move from the arms of the chair. She thought, *If you cry now, I swear I will never come back;* she had not forgotten the way he had seduced her with his tears in the past.

But Dean did not cry; on the contrary, he seemed quite content. And seeing him happy (though she suspected that he could not sustain it in the long run; his romantic nature canceled out long-term happiness; it is romance and cynicism that are hand in glove, not romance and happiness) won her back.

In the gathering darkness Em tries to tell herself that Dean has been detained at school, but she knows he is somewhere with Constance. She marches upstairs and begins to throw her things into a valise. She cannot quite believe that at age sixty-three she is finally going to leave him. The humiliation of having to see Constance in the quilting circle and Dean insisting that there is nothing more than friendship between them has become too much to take. She tries calling their daughter, Inez, to tell her that she is coming up to stay with her. Inez, who now lives in a small, expensive house in

Mill Valley. She'll say, I only need a place to get my bearings.

No answer. Em looks at her watch, sits on the bed, impatiently jerking her foot up and down. She had not told Inez that she and Dean were separated during much of her pregnancy. Or that Dean refused to have any more children once they had Inez. He said, "No. Out of the question. I can't imagine loving another child as much as I love Inez. I want to keep this pure." Pure? What the hell was *that* about, wonders Em for the millionth time, except more evidence of his selfishness: what Dean wants, not what she wants.

She wonders how Inez will take the news; her daughter, who seems to love both Em and Dean equally, adores them both. Dean proved to be a good father with an instinct for how much to give their child and what to withhold, so that she didn't go tearing out of their home like a bat out of hell as soon as she was old enough, like so many of the Grasse children.

Em tries Inez again—but still no answer. "I wish I smoked," she says aloud. Instead, she marches downstairs to pour herself a glass of white wine.

She remembers that she wants to take her silver Tiffany heart with her. Dean bought it for her on a trip they took to New York together, many years ago, a gift that came at the end of a great day of wandering around the city, going to the Frick and the Whitney and the Guggenheim. When they had lunch at the Café des Artistes and stood awestruck at the base of the Statue of Liberty. She has not worn it in years; and cannot now, with Constance in his life. Such a lie it would be. (She does not want to leave it here.) Dean lies.

But she cannot find it and, having exhausted the places where she thinks it will be, decides to check his studio.

Dean and Em have an express agreement that she not enter his studio when he is not there ("You can be so silly," she said), but today, with her impending hegira, she does not care. She feels she is not obligated to honor any agreements they have made; all between them is null and void. This is good-bye.

As she pushes the door open and walks straight over to the spindly bookcase that holds boxes, smooth stones, and bric-a-brac, as she goes to retrieve her heart, she stops for a final look around. It feels so decadent and rebellious being in Dean's place without Dean. It feels terrific and unfettered, like a lightness of spirit.

Dean's ideal project would be to paint someone's life from the cradle to the grave. And so he had begun with Em from the time right before they were married. Over against the wall, Em can see her engaged nineteen-year-old self with one of those funny perms from the forties, with only the bangs and tips of her hair curled, the rest left completely straight. Then she is twenty, wearing a white blouse with padded shoulders and an old pair of Dean's shorts, which fall to her knees, belted and bunched up at her small waist with a hand-tooled cowboy belt they picked up on their honeymoon in New Mexico. She remembers saying to him, "I don't want to be painted in this ugly old outfit. If you are going to paint me, I want to be beautiful."

"Exactly," he told her, then commanded her to stillness.

In another picture, there is strain in her brow: tiny, unhappy lines around her mouth from her discovery of Dean's infidelity. In another, she is heavy with child, reclining awkwardly on a divan, her skin alive with the glow of pregnancy and the renewal of her marriage (*Now*, thinks Em, *was I ever so radiant or is that just the artist's enhancement?*), and, if she's not mistaken, there is a slight swelling of her legs from water retention. Not long after that, she can be seen with her eyes cast down as she stands in a black cocktail dress and pearls.

There is Em with one-year-old Inez, dressed alike in mother-daughter outfits. Em loving Inez; Em draped in something gauzy, her face clean of makeup as she teeters on thirty; Em in an afternoon dress with hat and sunglasses. Em in the same sunglasses and naked. Em close to forty in a pose patterned after Goya's nude *maja* ("What was that again?" she asked Dean); Em in the garden; Em asleep; Em at fifty-two, with her hand to her brow.

Sometimes he painted the hollow of her throat; the repose of her hands; the directness of her glance; her hair mussed; her torso, focusing on her breasts and stomach, with a fine shading of hair that ended at her pubic line. She was clothed or naked; often not smiling or smiling small closed-mouthed smiles. He painted her feet; her flexed extended arm, fist closed like Charles Atlas; her sinewy back, with its minor muscle definition; her small waist; her buttocks, a little large, almost like animal haunches, with beginning pockmarks of fat toward the upper thigh; her legs angled so they looked better than they were. All these paintings of her various body parts. As if by dissecting his model, Dean could reconstruct her as he pleased or locate some essential center of her. Em could not decide, seeing these paintings now, as a whole, if this was love or loathing—this piecemeal approach to her person. One could say he dismembered her in this way so better to study, draw attention, or glorify each detail of her; as if his affection for her were so strong he could give it only in small doses to one part of her at a time. As if adoring her would surely overwhelm him.

It isn't as if she has never seen these paintings, but somehow, seeing them together this way, in her rather late middleage, almost carelessly placed about the studio, is sobering. On the one hand, she cannot recognize herself in any of them, cannot fathom that all these poses and pieces of Em are her. On the other hand, she marvels at how well Dean seems to know the many sides of her, taking care to document them all as if one day he will find himself without her, leaving behind only these myriad images.

What strikes her as well is what these perceptions of her reveal about Dean: eroticism, contentment, adoration, anger, possible danger, resentment, coolness. She finds herself saying to no one, *I swear he loves this woman,* as if it is not her, but another of Dean's Women. She suddenly knows that she cannot leave a man who knows her in this way. Cannot walk the world without him, seeing that she has to leave so much of herself behind. Sees how married they really are.

Em wanders back to their bedroom to unpack. Dean still has not returned. As she crosses to her closet, she becomes aware of the gentle swaying of a hanging plant, the shiver of the windows. Her bed-table lamp is beginning to jump and the fragile perfume bottles that sit atop her glass-top vanity are beginning to vibrate. She knows it is not a sonic boom but an earthquake. Em stands very still, in the center of the bedroom, contemplating moving to the doorway or curling up under her vanity, but earthquakes seldom frighten her and she always seems to spend the duration of them deciding the safest place to be without ever actually going there.

Then all is silent. It is over.

She feels a curious release after the quake, as if it has acted as some sort of circuit breaker in her psyche and now she can take a deep breath and start anew. It is not that she doesn't feel that initial sense of anxiety at the onset—she does—it is just that her apprehension seldom stirs her into action. She sometimes thinks she must be either very trusting or very stupid, but she always believes that she will emerge shaken but intact.

Her first thought is, *Where is Dean?*

But the rocking of the house ceases and all is quiet. She looks up to see Dean in the doorway, his face ashen and sadly in love.

Dean was not what the circle called a "decent man."

But he had pockets of goodness as well as anger, and Em finally thought him precious to her. How could she leave a man who knew her so thoroughly? That is what brings on confusion in people: this sense of wandering through the world, accompanied but unknown.

She cannot abide the company he keeps with Constance and she cannot quit him. Em will contribute yellow roses and silver hearts to the upcoming *Crazy Quilt. I call it Chickie's Garden,* Constance said to Marianna.

She cannot quit him. Will he never cease to be the child who cries to hold the moon?

Instructions No. 5

WAITING. THE WORST DREAM OF THE NIGHT, WHEN you are parted from someone you love and you do not know exactly where he is but you know he is in the presence of danger. You are suspended in a state of ignorance and worry and fear. It can tear you apart like the razor teeth of a sudden beast. You are tormented by a desire to keep the one you love safe. But he may be in a far-off land, fighting a good war like World War II or an undeclared war like the Vietnam War. It makes no difference to you; these conflicts call forth men you have given birth to, men you have married, men who have fathered you. The men fight. The women wait. It takes the patience of Job.

A quilt should be kept clean and properly stored when not on display or in use. Plastic for long periods of storage is discouraged; it is better to use special acid-free wrapping paper. The sort that might hold a wedding gown long after the ceremony. It may be purchased through a firm in New York City.

Watch for water stains or damage due to rodents

147

or moths. The problem is, you may not know when these elements or beasts threaten your quilt. You could be making dinner for your family or straightening up the front room or hosing down the garden or doing your part for the war effort in a munitions factory. You could be buying gasoline with your rationing card. All the while blissfully innocent of the risk to your quilt. You could believe it safe in an upstairs closet, attic, or basement. You have done everything the books say to store it properly, to keep it safe from harm. Yet it may not be safe.

Do not use bleach. The strong chemical will disintegrate your quilt before your very eyes and you will have to explain to your aunt or mother or friend what happened to the quilt she gave you on the occasion of your birth, wedding, Christmas. But you know how chemicals can destroy things. Mustard gas cut a swath of permanent damage in veterans of the Great War; Agent Orange left its mark on the veterans of Vietnam.

Be gentle in your cleansing regime and keep in mind that it does the quilt no good at all to remain dirty, even slightly. Strike a delicate balance in its care. It is likely that with all your precautions your quilt will still show signs of age. Do not be alarmed. This is part of the life cycle of cloth fibers.

Set to dry on a flat surface or shower rack, if space is a problem. Extremes of temperature can affect the improperly stored quilt, specifically, heat. You understand that the jungles of Southeast Asia can be brutally hot and moist. You may notice some discoloration.

An experienced dry cleaner can sometimes help

you with the problem of quilt cleaning. Remember, when doing it yourself, always test the cloth first by rubbing a modest amount of cleaning solution on a small bit of the material. Some colors or threads may run. Watch for this.

Always rinse in clear, cool water.

And remember, no matter how careful you are, you might not be able to prevent some damage to your quilt—no matter how attached you are to it, or how much of your skill and time you have invested in it or how carefully you followed all the rules for care, something unforeseen may ruin it beyond repair, leaving only the memory of the quilt behind. Do not castigate yourself; you may not be to blame. You did your best. These are fragile textiles. These things happen.

Waiting. During the forties the women left the sphere of the home to fill in the void left by the men (now soldiers) in munitions factories or sitting in the lonely booth of a railroad switchyard. For the first time, outside jobs were held by married women, not just the young or single or poor. An increase of 57 percent. Still. There were no women doctors; no women making top-level decisions; no equal pay. And when the men came home, it was back to the house, where you were encouraged to find new dinner recipes, oversee homework of the children you were asked to give birth to—children who needed mothers waiting for them when they came home from school, husbands who expected wives to be standing at the door, martini in hand for them, the smells of supper filling the house. This vigilance of women for their families.

What no one told you about those boy children you bore was that they would one day be taken from you as your husbands once were; these boys were only on loan to you.

The popularity of quilting rises in periods of war: tailored to the Revolutionary War; recording the Civil War with its loss of 600,000 lives; the quilts that bear Victory signs or the names of kin lost in battles, locally or in places far away that you have never seen. When war was declared on December 8, 1941, the sole dissenting vote was cast by Jeanette Rankin (R) Montana (who did the same for World War I). A woman, perhaps, tired of waiting.

The newest quilt is the Names Quilt, representing those Americans who have died youthful deaths from an incurable disease. This quilt is eclectic in its beauty (consider that America is the great melting pot and no two deceased are alike), staggering in its implication of waste. It covers nine acres and bears nine thousand names. Say it slowly: nine thousand. There are towns speckling the United States with populations of a few thousand. Grasse is barely four thousand strong. A farmer can easily make a living off nine thousand acres of cotton or wheat or strawberries or citrus. The quilt weighs tons. Cloth, thread, appliqués individually weigh next to nothing but combined, bearing nine thousand patches, it is a heavy burden. It has the capacity to crush. It originally began as a 3 × 6–foot patch. Wonder at and decry its weight gain and growth; insist that it should have been stopped at, say, thirty pounds. Express outrage that it ever grew to one hundred pounds. Be grief-stricken that it represents only 20 percent of those deceased, does not even begin to measure those afflicted. It is a waiting disease. But all this may be too sad to contemplate if you are a beginner.

Consider these items:

A quilt overseen by a northern woman called Cornelia Dow, whose husband served in the Union Army, had inked this onto her quilt: *While our fingers guide the needles, our thoughts are intense (in tents).*

Regarding one of many quilting fairs to raise money for the war effort, Abraham Lincoln said: "I have never studied the art of paying compliments to women; but I must say, that if all that has been said by orators and poets since the creation of the world in praise of women were applied to the women of America, it would not do them justice for their conduct during this war. . . . God bless the women of America."

Louisa S. McCord wrote to Mary Chesnut at the end of December 1862—Mary Chesnut, whose husband held a prominent place in the Confederate government and could be seen having dinner with Jeff Davis himself—regarding the death of her son, a Confederate soldier: *I cannot write more, but only to thank yourself and Colonel Chesnut for your efforts to help my darling. It is all over now, and it is right perhaps that the country will never know how much it has lost in my glorious boy.* You know both sides, righteous and false, can feel loss at war. And you have no doubt that Mrs. McCord put in her time waiting for him. Busied herself waiting for word of him.

There are quilts that record and pay respect to the

battles of a husband or lover or father or son. Battle after battle, across time, recorded, set down for posterity. Because it is immoral to forget. These things are not glorified, just recorded. Tattooed on the heart; burned into the family's history. This piecing together of the life of your child; this homage; this attempt to put it all in order; and even though you will one day wish for the heartbreak to leave you, it never will.

Outdoors

CORRINA AMURRI AND HY DODD GO BACK MANY years. Their boys, Laury and Will, were born only a few months apart. The women gave each other baby showers, had coffee together in the calm mid-morning hours of the weekdays, alternated lunch-times at each other's homes, traded baby-sitting services. Quilted together at Glady Joe's.

Laury and Will were not initially fond of each other, but their parents' friendship drew them closer, sometimes jokingly referring to each other as broth-ers. Both boys had siblings, younger, but they shared the brotherhood of the firstborn, which can be both blessing and curse; the overwhelming adult attention to the details of their lives and development; the ex-pectations that run too high; being the bridge be-tween adults (parents) and children (siblings); one foot in either place and the accompanying hollow, lonely feeling of belonging nowhere. Sometimes the oldest child is the lost child. Both parents and chil-dren recognize this, and it serves to make the oldest child's tragedies a little sweeter and more poignant than the younger children's similar experiences.

153

The oldest child is unsure, always. It is uncertainty that comes from charting out new territory, dragging his parents along, clearing the way for siblings.

When one makes a pancake, one always makes a tester first: the one that is poured on the hot griddle, then discarded as imperfect. Someone once said that oldest children are like tester pancakes and should be tossed out. It was Hy who said that.

They are buried children, locking up their rebellious or unruly nature, sometimes taking it out on brothers and sisters, hiding it from the adults. They bury the insecurity, the need; they overachieve or they disappear; they often harbor just the smallest fear. So fragile, really, said Corrina, the way they swagger and act as though they are responsible only for themselves in the world.

Will and Laury were fundamentally different, but they shared the understanding of the oldest child.

Will Dodd wanted to be an artist like Em's husband, Dean, who taught him to paint in school. He loved his family (fell prey to the oldest child's conflict of obligation and rebellion), but was anxious to be done with Grasse, a place he saw as intolerant of eccentricity or personal differences. He saw it as an essentially petty, cruel, nosy community, quick to ostracize and judge.

Laury loved his small town and his family. He loved the heavy winter tule fog, the occasional light powdering of snow, and the summers hot as blazes. He seldom felt so much himself as he did in Grasse. To him, the community was protective and understanding, watching out for one another, helping if there was trouble. All the children belonged to the adults; each mishap shared by all families.

The citizens of Grasse amused Laury: people who could not make a scheme succeed or rich kids who never had to work and grew into adults who spent their lives cataloging butterflies (postcards, stamps, train sounds) or writing the town's history or building silly, vain monuments simply because they could afford to do so. Laury thought this funny, while Will scowled and said, "The waste it represents is obscene."

"Lighten up," said Laury.

Laury also loved the public swimming pool in the summer, liked to complain with other kids about the boredom of Grasse, liked working his summer job, where he ran into just about everyone he knew.

When Will and Laury turned eighteen, Will received a college deferment while Laury enlisted. Ever since the Civil War, the largest group of enlistees had hailed from the American South, lower- and working-class backgrounds and various minority groups. So the surprise was not Laury's enlistment, but Will's deferment.

Will said to Laury, I can't believe you buy into all that patriotic crap.

Laury said to Will, I'm not afraid to fight for my country.

Will said, Afraid? Did I say I was *afraid*?

Laury asked, Don't you think this is just the greatest place on earth to live? Didn't our fathers fight in World War II?

This ain't no Good War, friend, said Will.

But Laury said, I don't mind protecting something I love. Even you.

Which silenced Will, caused him to think, *But who is going to protect* you, *Laury?*

Corrina and her husband, Jack, are proud of their Laury, although Jack has feelings about the war that he has never confided to Corrina. He is not altogether sure that this conflict requires the attendance of his boy. Of anyone's boys. Corrina squeezes her husband's hand and says, "Jack, Laury's got to do what he thinks is right. I don't have to tell you." But Jack begins taking long, lonesome walks during which he can think about his oldest child in private. Alone in his fields, his fears are diffused, as if he were scattering them like seed across the grasslands.

When Jack is inside, enclosed in the warmth and intimacy of his home, his fear seems to gain in density and strength. During the hot weather, Jack takes to sleeping outdoors.

Corrina takes to painting their house. It is not unusual for people passing to see Corrina standing atop a short ladder in one of Jack's old shirts and paint-spattered overalls. When Hy comes over, she sits on the grass (sometimes bringing a blanket, lying in her bathing-suit top and skirt) and chats happily with Corrina. Mostly, they talk about Laury and Will.

Hy saying, You must be so proud of that boy.

Corrina saying, Yes, of course. But I think we'd be proud of him whatever he decided to do.

Then Hy replies, If that is a reference to Will, you don't need to mind my feelings. Away at that college, we just don't know what the hell he is up to. We hardly ever hear from him.

And Corrina says something like, Joe is participating in a debate next Thursday, would you like to go with us?

Hy says yes, she'd love to, and does he miss his older brother very much?

Very much, says Corrina. She only brought up Joe to change the subject because she does not want to tell Hy that Will occasionally calls her during the day. And once, late at night, when he sounded drunk and it was lucky Corrina answered the phone and not Jack, who, she is sure, would have lectured him, then told the Dodds about it. Corrina is reasonably certain that Will does not want his parents to know he calls Corrina and Corrina feels no compulsion to tell them either. She thinks Will must know that about her.

When Corrina finishes painting the exterior of the house, she begins making plans to lay new linoleum in the kitchen. "But this is perfectly fine," insists Jack.

Corrina only pats his cheek in passing, as she measures out the dimensions by placing one foot over the other. Jack catches her hand, midair, as she pulls it away, and he puts it back to his face. He holds it across his mouth, and for a split second Corrina thinks he may start to cry. Only he doesn't. He shuts his eyes tightly.

★ ★ ★

Every night Corrina, Jack, and Joe watch the evening news with a kind of fixated horror. It is always during suppertime and they each find it personally amazing that they have learned to eat and watch at the same time. Each night they convince themselves that Laury is not a statistic in the casualty run-down. That he remains their living, faraway child. Their baby.

There are nights that Corrina wants to join Jack, sleeping outside, but she does not want to leave her house. She feels as if she can only keep her worrying about Laury under control if she can keep her home intact. But one night she does wander out to where Jack is lying on a chaise lounge. She wraps herself in a blanket and fits her body beside his.

"Come back inside, honey," says Corrina.

"In a minute," answers Jack.

"Look, he's all right."

"I miss him, Cor. I'm scared," he tells her.

"Just come inside," she says, tugging on his sweater as if to physically bring him with her.

Corrina has the phone cradled beneath her chin as she measures the new curtains while talking to Will.

"Tell me again why you aren't in class right now. For god's sake, Will, it's the middle of the day."

"They're having a protest. About the curriculum. You know."

"Oh, what, the administration building under

siege?" Her words are garbled because she is holding a chalk pencil between her teeth.

"Yeah," says Will, "something like that."

"Why aren't you there?" asks Corrina.

"I don't know . . . it's not my thing. . . . I mean, they have a point but it's just not my thing." Will cups his hand over the receiver and Corrina hears him say, "In a minute, man."

"Do you have to go?" She wishes they could end this soon. She really wants to get to these drapes.

"No," says Will, then, "yeah, I do. But I'll call you soon, okay?"

"Bye, Will."

"Later."

Corrina thinks it's funny that Will calls her. It isn't as if they ever talk about anything important or exchange secrets or, well, *anything*. And each time she has the sense that he is finally about to get to the point, to reveal his true reason for his phone calls—as if all these small, inconsequential ones are leading up to the Real Call. If only she wasn't so busy with these drapes, she could sit down and write him a letter.

Joe is lying on the ground next to Jack, who is in his customary lounge, but without a covering; a good indication he will not be sleeping outside tonight. Jack is thinking that he and Corrina spend so little time with Joe, who, at fifteen, has his own life but is still not entirely grown up. Jack can tell when he sees the excitement in Joe's face when he says that he and Corrina will be at the debate.

But Corrina is so busy lately. Reupholstering the

sofa, retiling and grouting the upstairs bathroom, and he believes that he heard her saying something to Joe about wallpapering his bedroom, to which Joe replied, "Mom, everything is just the way I like it."

"But nothing stays the same, honey," said Corrina.

Jack wishes he could be as industrious as his wife; instead he feels lethargic, soporific, as if he simply doesn't have the energy that his life requires anymore. He guesses he is getting old.

Poor Joe. Standing between a mother devoted, literally devoted, to her house and a father who suffocates at the thought of it.

At the time it seemed like a mistake not to marry Jack before he went to Europe to fight. Corrina took a job as a switchman for the railroad in Kern County, even though it meant long hours without seeing anyone except the waving hand of an engineer as he maneuvered his train from one track to another. She wore Jack's old shirts to work, the same ones she put on to clean the house or read the newspaper, with its articles concerning the war effort and what all of us at home could do for our boys. Already two of her girlfriends had moved to Long Beach, doing assembly work. The pay was "pretty good, better than home," and they urged her to come and join them.

No, she told them—she had to wait for Jack. He left her in Grasse and she wanted him to know that she was exactly where he left her. She could not possibly disrupt her life when his was so chaotic and uncertain. How would he feel getting a letter from her with a Los Angeles return address, a place not her parents' home? Of course, if she told him that it was for the war effort, he would understand; but she was superstitious and had invented a structure where her life would remain unchanged in his absence so that when the war ended he could simply slip back into it, as if he had never left her at all.

Then Laury became an MIA. Jack made an ugly confession to Corrina: "Cor, I know I'll be forgiven for saying this, but I hope our boy is never taken into an enemy prison."

"You don't mean it," said Corrina. How could he say this, knowing Laury was missing? The gentle art of waiting and patience. Jack had no patience; he was new at this. "If he is taken prisoner, we'll get him back."

"No, it is better to be killed. No one survives prison, even civilian ones. Physically, yes, but deep inside—I don't want Laury home and gone at the same time." Jack had formulated this thought during his wanderings, when his fear was diffuse and manageable. *After all,* reasoned Jack, *I can scarcely tolerate the terror of being inside my own home; how is Laury going to survive a prison camp?*

So Corrina spent her days and every third weekend (including the nights) in the switch house. She was allowed to listen to the radio and write letters. She saved her money to pay for the trip to Paris that she and Jack would take someday. His letter said, *Paris is incredible, wonderful, it's tops. Despite all it's been through. It calls you to my mind.* And: *I want you to see the Eiffel Tower. It looks like iron lace, unfinished, piercing the sky. It looks like the structure of something it means to be one day. I want to stand with you at its peak.*

Jack sent her a pair of ivory-and-silver earrings that looked very old, as if they had been passed down. And a pocketbook made of imitation leather.

He talked about the "great guys" he was meeting (she reads this in the solitude of her job), from all over the United States. He even met a couple of expatriates, who told him that they could not help but see Spain, France, and Germany in a different, confusing way. The expatriates felt differently about America, too, though Jack was not clear as to what they meant by that. He wrote her that the bread was unlike any he had ever had before, heavy, crusty, rich; the wine not too unlike California wine—though he had to admit he was hard put to tell the difference. *They say my palate is too American.*

What he did not discuss in his letters to Corrina was what he saw when his regiment liberated one of the concentration camps. He moved as if in a daze, as if he were looking through a window to another universe that resembled the earth and its inhabitants, but not quite. These people they found did not seem like the same species, their humanity transformed by their suffering and hollowness, making him feel foreign and embarrassed standing before them in his own good health. He could not properly identify the smell that skirted the camp.

Jack threw up behind a barrack. He was assailed by a gamut of emotions: He wanted to rush from this place, find a woman, make love to her, hold her close, and keep her safe. He wanted to gorge himself on food or void his bowels or sleep for twenty-four hours or run to the point of exhaustion. Witnessing the deprivation here, he was moved to excess.

As he stood, wiping his mouth, eyes, and nose on his sleeve, removing all traces of sickness, he wondered, *Is this what the absence of God looks like?* He could not believe that God did not exist—even with this vision before him—as much as it seemed that He had decided, inexplicably, to go underground for a while. *If someone described this to me, I would not believe it,* because he could not believe that God would watch and not act; he could not accept that.

Again, he was overwhelmed by the desire to caress a woman, push himself up inside her until his entire self was buried within her womb and he could be reborn innocent, pure, never having witnessed this at all.

Corrina did not pray for Laury. She had prayed before, when Jack was overseas. Her reserve of patience had been used up when Jack was in Europe; none was left for Laury, who remained unheard from. She could not pray because she wanted to shake her fist at God, at the unfairness of being forced through the ordeal of waiting for a soldier, not once in her life, but twice. She wanted to scream, How much am I supposed to endure? And because she questioned God, she could not ask for His blessing. Perhaps this was the curse of Eve.

Still, she went to church on Sunday with Jack and Joe; but she spent silent time, with head bowed, accusing and bartering with God and not really praying.

Jack, too, was aware that he was less than sympathetic to the war, but he would not show this to the citizens of Grasse, who regularly asked about Laury. It would not stand right with them and then there would be an argument and he could not argue something that held his boy in such danger.

He would prefer not to go to church with Corrina and Joe, but he would never mention this either. After his own experience in the war, he had been in conflict over his belief in God, unable to come to any resolution. He understood that the nature of spiritual faith calls for uncertainty, testing, and renewal, but the image of those prisoners seemed a greater testament to negligence than he could explain. And now that his own son was probably a prisoner somewhere, he could not help but see those scenes in vivid relief, Laury's face in each captive.

When James and Hy Dodd open their front door to Corrina and Jack Amurri, they reach their hands out to them, as if to draw them into the house, as if they would be reluctant to enter if left to their own prerogatives. Corrina steps in before Jack, while Jack follows wearing the cool air on his overcoat. Corrina and Jack stand, as always, with a slight space between them, as if they are careful to leave it open in case their child would be back any minute to fill it, bring them closer again.

After they exchange social amenities, Hy says, "We wanted to tell you we never stop thinking about Laury. You must admire him."

"Not like me," says Will, who steps out from behind his father to quickly kiss Corrina's cheek, dodging her hand before it comes to rest on his thin arm.

"He's a little distraught," confides Hy as Will leaves the room, to which James says, "We don't know what the hell he does at that college of his and *art*—how do you major in *art*? What is the point of going to college if you are going to study art?"

It is clear to Corrina that Hy and James are puzzled, embarrassed, and displeased that Will has a college deferment and is using it to study something that seems like fluff. They can't even say, "Well, he is going to be a doctor or engineer or architect." No, out of the war and into art.

"We suspect," Hy's voice lowers, "drug use."

"Now, we don't know that, Hy," says James abruptly.

"Of course," says Hy, absentmindedly rubbing her husband's arm. "You're right." But it has crossed Corrina's mind as well. It's all one hears about these days, and he is in school up at San Francisco State, with all those other students and their protests (*Not my thing,* he had told her during one of their phone conversations) and free love and doing whatever the hell they feel like doing when they feel like doing it, and none of them even knows her boy's name.

Then, awkwardly, from James: "Corrina, Jack—look, about Laury, we heard—"

"And they want to tell you they wish I was half the man Laury is," calls Will from the other room.

"Will—" says James roughly as Hy shakes her head and he stops. Just stops. It occurs to Corrina that she is witnessing Hy and James's disapproval of Will mixed with the relief that, while he may be turning into some uncontrollable, disrespectful stranger, at least he is here. He is home and not in some foreign country fighting people who don't even speak English. Or maybe that does not cross their minds at all; maybe that only occurs to her. And she tries to be fair—to ask herself which is worse, a son like Will, who comes home only grudgingly to treat his parents with undisguised contempt (and might be taking drugs), or one like Laury, doing the right thing in a distant land with names that she could not even pronounce until she heard them repeated daily on the television.

Corrina knows the answer: It is better to have him home. It is better to have him close.

Will looks terrible; long hair falling over his shirt collar, generally unwashed and unkempt-looking. Even his younger sister Gina seems to pull away from him. Gina is at the silent and sullen age of fifteen and appears to suffer all these adults and her awful brother. Gina bears no "hippie" trappings, instead looks like a fashionable young girl who pores over teen magazines (BEAUTY TIPS TO MAKE HIM SAY *WOW*). She tucks her long hair behind one ear with a bored sigh as she picks at her dinner.

Will whispers something in her ear, which she answers by saying, "Oh, shut *up*."

Hy is saying that a couple of girls from school are constantly calling him. "Imagine," says Hy, "could you see *us* calling boys when we were their age?" To which Corrina remarks, "We were practically married at their age." Elicits a snort of laughter from Will. Corrina wonders about a girl that Will told her he was seeing. She asked him about it when he stopped mentioning her name; recalls his unhappy voice when he said, "Look, we don't *own* each other. She can do what she likes."

Will's jeans are worn and faded, patched over with flower appliqués, peace signs, and angry, raised fists. He is sharply aware of all that goes on around him, despite the neglect of his appearance. As they make small talk at dinner, Corrina looks from Hy to James, her eyes crossing the distance between the two by way of Will, only to notice him openly staring at her.

Corrina can see, clearly, that he understands the waste of this polite conversation and the trouble she is having controlling what she really wants to say, which is that Will is *here* and Laury is *there* and there seems to be no love in the world because she had waited for Jack years ago as a lover and is now forced to wait for Laury as a mother. How she spent such long, desperate hours in the switch house, her anxiety bubbling so close to the surface that she terrified herself. And how these days, all she can do is tear apart and restore her house, with fury and with hope.

"I waited for Jack," Corrina blurts out over desert.

"Yes," says Hy, confused, both hands holding her coffee cup midway between the table and her mouth.

"During the war," she says, "I waited. I was a good girl. No one heard me cry because I didn't cry, because I was so patient."

"We all were," says Hy.

"But, you see," says Corrina, "I hated every goddamn minute of it."

Corrina excuses herself, appears as if she is going to the bathroom, but heads out to the garden instead. As she passes through the kitchen she notices the empty cocktail glasses that Hy set next to the sink to be rinsed. Corrina extracts one that is still half full, with melted ice cubes and a twist of lime rind floating along the top, pungent with the smell of gin. And heads outside.

The glass is cold and sweating from the ice. She takes a long sip; her nose wrinkles at the diluted taste of gin, tonic, and ice. The sweet smell of a marijuana cigarette drifts in her direction; she turns to see Will drop his cupped hand, slightly turned from her. Corrina lowers herself into the cushions of the redwood lawn furniture and takes another swallow of the drink.

"It doesn't matter to me. Really." She leans her head back as Will relaxes, openly drawing on the rolled cigarette. "I know it's illegal," she says, "but there are legal things that are much worse."

"Yeah, right," says Will, settling in the chair beside her.

"The draft, for example, is legal. That's not such a good thing. Wouldn't you agree that it's not such a good thing?" She holds her glass with her fingertips, palm over the top, spider-style. "Of course you would" (she says as she nods). "After all—I don't mean to insult you—but you aren't there, now are you?"

"No, Corrina, I'm not. You have that one hundred percent correct." Will has taken a roach clip from his front pocket and is pinching the stub of the joint with it. "Damn," he says as the light goes out. He fumbles in his pockets for matches.

Corrina says, "I'd like to help you out but I don't have any on me," then spreads her arms wide as if to prove her claim. "Ah, I am so comfortable. Do you ever sleep out here?"

Will is on his feet, reaching in his back pockets. "No. Never."

"Not even in hot weather?"

He walks over to the barbecue grill, removes a long wooden match from a brightly decorated box. It has a turquoise tip. "Never."

"Your parents?"

"Huh?" asks Will, looking up, glancing toward the house, half afraid, half defiant.

"I said, Do your parents ever sleep outdoors?" Corrina rests her elbow on the wide arm of the lounge, turning her body to see Will attempting to light that small bit of marijuana and paper with a ridiculously long match.

"Damn," he says, pulling his face away quickly, as

if burned. He again opens the tall box, extracting another match, this one with a purple tip. "I'm sorry? My parents? No, they don't. At least not that I know of."

"Ah, then it's only Jack," Corrina whispers, prompting Will to look up and ask, "What was that, Corrina?"

"No need, I suppose," then louder: "When did you stop calling me Aunt Corrina?"

Will has finally lit the roach and is taking a deep pull on it as he resumes his place beside her. He holds the cigarette out to her, but she shakes her head, swishes the liquor in her glass. "I don't know. When I grew up, I guess."

"But you are barely twenty. A baby."

"Maybe when I discovered that you are the only adult I can halfway stand these days." He stops. "Look, there were a couple of times I slept out here. Me and Laury. We used to call it torture camping because it was either too cold or too bug-ridden or too wet or too boring. Torture camping." He wets his fingertips, tamps out the rest of the joint. "I'd forgotten about it."

Corrina looks away, pours the remainder of the drink from her glass, splashing the concrete patio. "Laury," she whispers.

"I write him letters," Will says suddenly. "I tell him what I am doing, I tell him I talk to you. I tell him to get the fuck out of there. I never send them; I call you instead. I talk to you. You know, Corrina, I don't approve of the war. My parents don't understand that—that I simply don't approve."

"Neither do I," says Corrina, "approve of the war."

"But something else," says Will, taking a deep breath. "I just never mention Laury's name. And it isn't that he could be me and I could be him. We fought before he left. So honor bright; not like me, bad old Will, whose parents wish he'd go away and stay there. Even Gina gives me grief. I am the family disgrace.

"Anyway, I want to tell you that I don't talk about him because I feel . . . I don't know . . . a little lost without him. Incomplete. Like I need to check in with him. Ah. My honorable half. So I can't talk about him and I can't worry about him. Fuck—the only thing I can do is miss him. And be angry with him."

"Me, too," says Corrina. "I miss him, too."

Jack comes out looking for Corrina, who is already standing, readying herself to reenter the house, but wishing she could stay on the cool patio "a little longer. I know I'd feel better," but smiles broadly when she spies Jack, who asks, "Are you feeling okay?" then turns angrily to Will and says, "You reek. You are a disgrace."

This causes Will to laugh. "I certainly am that. Why, I was just saying to Corrina that I am real persona non grata around these parts."

Jack wraps an arm around his wife, as if he is shielding her from Will's bad influence. But Corrina has started crying and is balking at the idea of returning to the inside of the house. "Honey," she says to Jack, "I really can't go in there. Not inside.

You know what I mean. So, let's just go around through the gate and walk home."

"But we have to say good-bye," Jack reminds her gently.

"Oh, no, no, they'll understand. Really."

"What about the car?" asks Jack.

Corrina quietly considers this, then says brightly, "Will. Will can be trusted. You'll drive it back for us, won't you?" She feels Jack tense up but says, "You better say yes, Jack, because I am not getting into any car tonight. I truly am not."

Jack hesitates, takes in the smirk on Will's face, says, "Honey, I'll come back for it tomorrow."

"That would be fine," says Corrina. "We have to go home now." She kisses Will on the cheek. "Good-bye."

Will holds her hand a little longer than he should, pats her on the back as she turns to leave.

"I don't think much of you at all," hisses Jack.

Will nods his head. "Yes, yes. That is no secret."

But as it was, Laury was killed, not taken prisoner. And years later, when all those living boys were coming home in defeat, Jack and Corrina took a long trip to Pendleton, their fingers wrapped around the links of the metal fence, fiercely; they dare not let go.

Instructions No. 6

THERE IS A SOUTH AFRICAN MYTH REGARDING A BE-
ing called *Sikhamba-nge-nyanga*, which translated
means "She-who-walks-by-moonlight." This is
what is said of her: *It is man's privilege to gaze upon
her.* But when he violates *the customs which protect and
nourish her, she returns to nature.* In order to ensure
her survival, she must be allowed to walk freely, un-
touched and unmolested.

A Guyanese story says of black slaves that the
only way they can be delivered from "massa's
clutch" is to *see the extra brightness of the moon in
their lives. The darkness will always be there, but they
can use the light of the moon as hope.* The light of the
moon. The dancing buffalo gal with the hole in her
stocking.

One can survive without liberation but one cannot live without freedom. You know it is essential
to find one's freedom.

Here are some things you know:

That the English adopted slavery from the Spanish. Found it useful when the white English were
no longer motivated to come to the New World.

173

Some masters were unnecessarily cruel, running their "investments" into the ground (you are appalled to learn that in Brazil and the Caribbean this was considered sound business sense). Squeezing every drop. Other masters were benevolent, treating their slaves with a modicum of kindness. Of course, words like *kindness* and *fairness* lose all meaning in a labor system founded on the purchase of human flesh, based on involuntary bondage. To paraphrase a Famous Writer: A master is a master is a master.

Female slaveholders are called mistresses.

A sewing slave in the antebellum South could be had for $1,800. Anything less would be a steal—worth gloating over with the neighboring slaveholders. You get the idea.

Most slave owners did not have fancy Taras and owned just one or two slaves. This meant a female slave could work in the fields all day, only to fill her nights with mountains of sewing and quilting for the family. A slave was fortunate to be in a household that allowed her specialized work like sewing, exclusively. But a word like *fortunate* tends to lose its meaning in a context such as this.

You personally find the piecing together of the work tedious—arduous and dull. Likewise for cutting the pieces, securing the batting between the back and top work. But you find the designing and creation of the quilt theme exhilarating. As if you are talking beauty with your hands. Make yourself heard in a wild profusion of colors, shapes, themes, and dreams with your fingertips. The tedium of quilt construction some days can make you cry; you long to express yourself. To shout out loud in silk and bits of old scarves.

You know that it was not uncommon during the Depression for a wealthy woman to hire out to a poor woman the drudgery of quilting. And that that same wealthy woman could still enter that quilt in a competition solely under her name—no thank-you or acknowledgment to anyone else.

You hold no stock in the prefab, purchased-pattern quilt. You do not understand the point of stitching without your own heart-involvement. Without your ideas incorporated into the work, it is just an exercise, something to fill the long evening spent without companionship.

More things you know:

That only you can tell your story.

That most abolitionists were women striving for suffrage as well. That a significant number of abolitionists were prejudiced against the Negro they fought to free; it was the institution they considered immoral. So the word *free* begins to lose its meaning in a context such as this.

So little in your life has changed. Despite the civil rights movement. Here is an incident emblematic of that time: Myrlie Evers, the widow of Medgar Evers, wanted to tell President Kennedy, at the funeral of her much-loved husband, that she was devastated; that her husband fought for his country in World War II and came home to be a second-class citizen; that she was furious he had been murdered trying to secure his constitutional rights for himself and his people. But all she said, finally, when Kennedy asked her how she was doing, was *Fine, thank you, Mr. President*. This impresses you; this is something you understand without effort. That the story of your life and history should be so plain, so obvious, yet you will be asked to explain it. You, too, can imagine shrugging your shoulders or registering the same reaction to such an inquiry. This is what it is like with your quilts; you simply design and stitch them. You say nothing more than what you have said with fabric and thread.

Here is a glossary of some of the quilts you have designed:

Stars Like Diamonds: Beauty's hands fill with them, as she cries her disloyal tears. You think that tears of diamonds have no value when shed falsely. Embroider the tears with silver thread that was left over from an evening gown made for the lady of the house.

Winter Wheat: Do not use a repeating pattern but instead fill the pale blue field with thin, pliant stocks that undulate in the cool wind. Use blue denim, cotton, down, and flannel from farmer's clothing to comprise the wheat, earth, and sky. You are both drawn to and repelled by agriculture.

Pomegranate Fish: Dyed natural linen for texture, deep red-purple. Fish that swim in blue water; faceted beads of antique garnets circle your neck. Refracts sunlight, calls to mind your own mother, now gone.

Moving by the Light of the Moon: The moment he wanted you. You did not know him, nor did he know you. Even after, he did not know you. Batik cotton allows for the color of the moonlight through the trees. Indigo silk spans the night sky.

We all crave the human embrace. We cannot guard our hearts with vigilance.

The Life Before: Reminder of ancestors. What cannot be told to someone who does not want to listen or does not express curiosity. You feel better when you hold the story patches between your fingers. Use yarn, shredded curtain fabric, yards of amethyst satin.

Forest Leaves: A childhood quilt for your daughter. A great and powerful trunk surrounded by swirling leaves in hues of green: hunter, kelly, verdant, grass, dark-green-almost-black. Bull Connor turned hoses on protesters in Birmingham, with water pressure great enough to tear the bark from a tree, roll a small girl down the main street. Not for your child; not for Marianna. Leaves are appliqué.

Broken Star: Traditional pattern made from print fabric on a field of peach. You wanted to study the stars. They made you feel whole. The quilting pattern is of tiny hawk moons.

Blue Moon: That which is rare and hopeful. Comes along when it is the second full moon within the same month. More indigo. Appliqué a Spanish fan hovering in the sky. With trails of gold and scarlet, as if flung by a dancer.

Friendship Across Time and Distance: Many colors, dyed cotton, scraps of royal-blue velvet, heart of pink muslin. Understand that friendship arrives from the least likely sources and flourishes in the least likely locations. Understand that someone can know you very well though you have not told her about yourself. The base is from bleached white and amber cloth.

Many Shoes: Also for your daughter. Sarah Grimké said, *May the points of our needles prick the slave owners' conscience.* And a quilted needle book made to look like shoes said, *Trample not on the oppressed.* Your daughter will not be trampled upon. Your daughter will travel distances.

A Profusion of Hearts: Pale red satin; appliqués of wings and wheat fields shine golden across the work. This is a moment of love made for Pauline, Marianna, Glady Joe. Imported Chinese embroidery thread; you did all the work on this quilt alone, beginning to end. The tedious next to the inspired. It never felt like work.

When you embark upon a quilting project, you must decide between traditionally American designs using print fabric and the Amish or Hawaiian style of solid blocks, appliquéd in contrasting colors. You are philosophically drawn to the Hawaiian way, because they believe it is bad luck to appropriate another's design, to tell another's story. Hawaiian women learned quilting from white Christian missionaries. Before the missionaries arrived, the Hawaiians had their own way of making garments, which left no excess material. Nothing with which to make a quilt.

The Hawaiian women shunned the quilting bee as soon as they were proficient in the skill, preferring solitude and secrecy. You know in your own life that the quilt made solely by your hand, beginning to end, is very different from those made at

Glady Joe's house. Even down to the length of the stitches.

You should share the work but not the idea behind it. You understand this. But in a small, close circle it is difficult to do this. You trust the Hawaiian notion that to share your personal pattern is to share your soul. To compromise your power.

You also understand the Hawaiian woman's perplexity with the concept of sewing and leaving remnants of excess material as well as her rejection of group quilting. (Another concept introduced by the Christian missionaries.) You comprehend that need for solitude. Or for a handmade garment to use all the cloth with nothing left over.

And it seems to you a good idea to limit your "sharing" with the other women, and expect they should see that, too, with you. Do not share.

Many years ago a visitor to Hawaii bought two quilts, took them home to the mainland, copied their designs, and entered them under her own name in a contest. Which she won.

You are sad for the winner of the contest, because she "borrowed" someone else's story and fashioned it as her own. Sorry because she was rewarded by judges who did not understand that these quilts were not truly her own. The loss of power this entailed on the part of the Hawaiian woman; this loss of her history by having another woman appropriate it, in turn, increasing the second woman's already estimable social strength through stealing these designs. Increasing her own power. On your back. At your expense. You feel it most profoundly.

Tears Like
Diamond Stars

TO KNOW MY STORY, THINKS ANNA NEALE, IS TO understand my superimposition on the world, to see that I am in the world as shadow, as film laid upon the more vibrant picture. All underneath my image are people with families, children, husbands, houses, college degrees; all of one color. I am placed upon them as an architect uses an overlay sheet to illustrate the details of the structure he will build—and just as quickly, the overlay sheet can be again lifted, removing all traces of detail, leaving the bare structure.

I refused, at an early age, to be a specter in my own world. I decided that I would not be whisked away, so I sought to anchor myself to society, to make them see *me*, Anna Neale, child of a black mother (deceased) and a white father (whereabouts unknown and unacknowledged); gave birth to one child, my daughter, Marianna Neale; became undisputed leader and founder of the Grasse Quilting Circle (recognized nationally for superior and original work). Of course I know that outside of the quilting world, the Grasse women remain unknown. But I am not invisible because of this closed circle; I am not unknown. I learned to speak with needle and thread long before society finally "gave" me a voice—as if society can give anyone a voice; it can only take a voice away.

Anna Neale wore a necklace of faceted antique garnets that belonged to her great-grandmother. It hung low on her thin child's neck and sometimes irritated her, getting in the way at inopportune moments. She would reach her two hands up to it, as if to tear it from her throat, but Pauline would tell her not to worry, that she would grow into it. "It is part of your legacy, honey. Don't threaten it."

Anna loved a quilt that had been made by her great-great-grandmother, called *The Life Before*. It was now in Pauline's care, but it was promised to Anna one day. Anna measured her height by lying flat upon it, stretching her hands and feet between the designated squares.

It was divided into fifteen large squares filled with appliquéd animals, birds, men of dark brown, hovering angels blowing trumpets, serpents as large as life, stars, the outsized sun, flaming candles of dripping wax. These were African scenes: animals with tusks, warriors clashing with spirits and themselves and beasts. Candles that burned upside down. Giant fish devouring unfortunate men, who tumbled from enormous balancing scales. The colors of dense, earthy tones; yellow stars blaze a midnight field; the unforgiving sun.

This was all before the ships and the block and the coffle. Before the mix of blood that no white family would acknowledge in its own house but could readily identify in a neighboring family. All this because one race did not have the decency to be ashamed of dealing in human flesh.

Again. The quilt as dream-desire placed against the reality of the world.

Anna lived with her great-aunt Pauline in a couple's house in San Francisco. The man had inherited enough money (making him not rich but "comfortable") so that he did not have to work and could, instead, pursue his interest in astronomy, with his telescope trained on the heavens and his charts and maps and volumes. Anna would examine the books in his study as Pauline picked up and dusted; she would make the connection between stars in the book and the overscaled stars in the quilt. "Pauline," Anna asked, pointing to an illustration, "is this Africa?"

Pauline glanced at the picture as she passed by. "No. The sky belongs to nobody. The sky is free." So different from the earth.

Pauline decided that she would send Anna to college; Anna, with her love of heavenly bodies, stars, and comets. The man of the house was forever showing things to Anna, happy to have anyone interested in his hobby. He would pull up a chair and place Anna upon it so she could look through the telescope. Pauline heard him tell her about the nature of the planets, introduce her to the cosmos. Someday, he said, we'll go see for ourselves. Anna answering that she will be the first on board, to which the man replied, laughing, Now, that is not likely, is it?

Pauline hated the man for saying that to Anna. She walked into the study and pulled Anna off the chair. Anna slapped her arm; Pauline shook her niece and said, "I'm getting you your own telescope. Your *own*." With Anna looking back over her shoulder, smiling at the man.

The mrs. of the house lusted after *The Life Before*. Pauline explained to her, "These are African stories, African dreams and myths," and so on, but the woman was excited by and only interested in the quilt, not the story behind it.

"A real beauty," she said. "How much?" The mrs. fingered its edges, laid her hands upon the appliqués, clicked her tongue at the craftsmanship, the sophistication and elegance of the work.

Pauline gently extracted it from the woman's grasp. "It's not for sale."

Not long after, Pauline overheard the mrs. telling her friends about *The Life Before*. She heard her say, "I've never seen anything quite like it. . . . No, I'm sure you haven't, either. . . . Oh, it is *very* different. There are some stories that even go along with it. . . . Well, I don't remember them offhand, but I could find out. . . ." Pauline ran to the kitchen, where Anna sat doing her homework; who looked at her aunt's frantic expression and asked, "What's wrong?"

Pauline shook her head. Continued to her room, where she tore the quilt from her bed and folded it inside scented blue paper. Stuffed it high above in the back of her closet. The mrs. so coveted her quilt that Pauline no longer trusted what she would or would not do. It was better to remove all temptation.

When Anna asked after it, Pauline told her, "I have put it aside, baby, saving it for you."

"I want to see it now," said Anna, suspicious that it wasn't set aside at all but given to someone else.

"No," said Pauline firmly, not wanting to release it from the sanctuary of the closet and into the world of the mrs. "You'll just have to believe what I say."

As Anna grew older, it became increasingly difficult for Pauline to enter her room, with its cut-out photographs and drawings of stars and planets pinned to the walls.

Pauline went to the mrs. and asked for $25 for the quilt. The mrs., whose husband was not involved in the stock market and was left relatively untouched by the recent crash, said, "Pauline, given current events, you can certainly understand that I don't have twenty-five dollars."

Pauline started from the room. The mrs. said, "I'll give you fifteen dollars."

Fifteen, thought Pauline. *Why, that is nothing! How can I release my quilt to someone who does not know its value, in any sense?* But Anna was more important. She was now thirteen; she was sheltered, clothed, and fed, but she needed things in this life beyond that. She should understand luxury, even small, inconsequential luxury. (Education is a luxury. Pauline scowls.) Everyone should have *something* beyond simply being alive. Besides, Anna was becoming an accomplished quilter in her own right and perhaps she could make something as beautiful as *The Life Before*.

"Twenty," said Pauline.

The mrs. turned up her palms. "What do you want me to say? Fifteen is the best I can do."

Pauline took in the mrs.'s new dress of lavender silk; her wrist bright with a ruby-and-pearl bracelet, a recent gift from her husband.

The sale made, Anna in tears, Pauline silent. Pauline again told the mrs. the stories represented on the quilt until the mrs. listened without listening and Pauline gave up. Anna refused any thought of a telescope now, leaving Pauline to ask the mrs. if she could buy back her quilt.

"Oh, no," said the mrs. "I couldn't. It is too much to part with. I'm sure you understand."

The mrs. hung it on the walls of her sitting room, where Pauline could see it as she cleaned the room. She would visit it and wonder how she ever grew to be so foolish, so miscalculating. How could she ever have thought that material things didn't really matter, that they were all equal and interchangeable and that you still could not take them with you when you died. Pauline was ashamed to admit how much she loved the quilt. *The Life Before.* As time passed, she would still visit the quilt, but she would not touch it. She no longer told the quilt's stories to anyone, not even to Anna, realizing that now Anna might not remember them to tell to her children. But without the quilt as illustration, it was probably better to lose them altogether. To Pauline's relief and dismay, the mrs. never repeated the stories to her friends, who often admired her purchase and asked if the mrs. thought Pauline could be persuaded to make one for them.

Pauline wants to laugh at them, call them stupid, and say, Don't you know that only you can tell your story? You can't buy someone else's life. Then she stops. Hears her own words. *Well,* she will say if the mrs.'s friends ask her, *the quilt isn't by my hand, in any case.* That is what she'll say to shut them up.

Anna at sixteen shows no interest in the stars. Not for years now. Nor does she freely converse with the man regarding his hobby. She does not look at the books in his study. She has removed the makeshift solar system from her walls. "I prefer them unadorned," she says to Pauline.

She knows that Pauline misses her quilt, mourns it in silence because a Christian woman is not supposed to feel longing or regret for worldly things. Being that things of the spirit will sustain us over things of the flesh. But Pauline is lost, distracted, and distanced by the theft of her history, appropriated by someone for whom the quilt is an ornamental object and nothing more. Anna knows that Pauline only offered it up to the mrs. to gain something else for her—only to realize too late that some things cannot be bartered. And that it was with clenched fists that Pauline conducted the sale. Knows that she parted with the wrong thing and that it cannot be undone.

Why couldn't Anna have both things? The quilt

and the telescope; her history and her future? Why were their lives always a series of choices that seemed to cancel each other out?

As for the mrs., Anna can scarcely stand to be in the same room with her, let alone the same house; is disturbed from being that close to anyone who could buy something like the quilt; who could be that unabashedly immoral.

Anna did not even say good-bye when, at the age of sixteen, she left San Francisco. Left without warning. Hit the road. The night before she said to Pauline, "It grieves me to see you like this."

"It grieves me, too," said Pauline.

Then Anna was gone.

And *The Life Before* was gone with her.

And it was with great pleasure that Pauline approached the mrs. that day, all comfort and humility, took her hand, and placed $15 in its palm. She closed the mrs.'s fist around it and said, "I'll make you another one."

But the mrs. shook her head and wailed, "I wanted *that* one."

It was with lightness of heart and step that Pauline went from the room. "Too bad," she said softly in the hall, out of the mrs.'s earshot. "I just feel *so* sorry for you."

Anna Neale went south to the outskirts of Bakersfield, where she became the maid of a rancher's wife. The ranch had two business partners: one in Texas (who also had another ranch) and one in Chicago (who thought of his investment as romantic, a boyhood fantasy of the Old West). Anna's employers had inherited their capital, then built upon it. Because they grew up privileged, they were accustomed to having servants and therefore treated them in the old-money style, that is, neither cruel nor kind, intimate nor distant. The servants were simply invisible.

New money sometimes exercises its social muscle on hired help, reminding the servants of what they are in order to reaffirm what the employers have risen to. (Years later, during the early fifties, Anna will see the movie *Beauty and the Beast*, by Cocteau. In this film, the invisible servants of the Beast's castle are portrayed by human arms holding candelabras or receiving garments, as well as eyes that see, carved into ornate fireplaces and chairs. Anna will say to her daughter, Marianna, "See, baby—that was my life on the ranch." When Beauty cried, as she sat perched on the edge of the Beast's deathbed, her tears transformed into diamonds, falling into her hands, dropping onto the Beast's inanimate form. This will be the most memorable part of the movie for Marianna, not the invisible servants.)

One summer, the son of the Chicago partner spent three months on the ranch, where he met and fell in love with Anna—or, perhaps, it was the idea of Anna—whom he could not marry even though this is America and we are all God's children, because Anna was a maid and she was black. Her garnet necklace no longer overwhelmed her frame as it had when she was a child; she was now seventeen, with the garnets just skimming her delicate collarbone, their many facets refracting in the sunlight.

She moved with a singular grace. The boy noticed her walking around the house and on her evening strolls, where he watched her watching the night sky.

It was the way in which she considered the evening star that made him want her. *Sikhamba-nge-nyanga.*

She-who-walks-by-moonlight.

It was natural that the invisible Anna should find herself curious about and attracted to the high visibility of the rich Chicago boy. She had never had a lover before and found his admiration to be both thrilling and frightening. She could not trust him, yet she was not cautious. Divided her heart between her desire to respond to his proffered love and her dislike, mistrust of his skin; her shy affection for a boy close to her own age and the potency of his social power; she was both suspicious and willing in the face of love.

(There was a duality of historical forces at work: the interplay of racial color, as well as the son of the man from Chicago and the maid of the house simply carrying out a traditional arrangement between the classes.)

The boy reached for her garnet beads, laid his hand on both her necklace and her neck. Where did you get these? he asked.

My great-grandmother, she said, covering his hand with hers—either to caress his fingers or shove them away—she could not have said. I've had them for as long as I can remember.

They glinted like diamonds in the light.

Sometimes he treated her as if she knew nothing, but she knew that he never bothered to ask her the right questions. Like about the rotation of the planets or the significance behind a meteor shower or the meaning of a blue moon or how to lay down the base for a quilt. He came to her room when everyone was away for the day; he sat familiarly on her bed as Anna slouched against the wall. Anna noted the way he examined each square of *The Life Before.* She held her breath; she thought he might ask the right questions.

"It has a name," she said, stepping closer.

"Is that so?"

"It's called *The Life Before.*" She felt suspended between airy heights and great depths.

"The Life Before," he repeated. Then asked, "Do you ever think about me?"

Anna relaxed her breathing. She decided to tell him the quilt stories (the ones that Pauline thought she might have forgotten) had he asked; he did not ask. And she saw herself as he might have seen her, as someone who did not matter to him, as something to do during his interim on the ranch. She reconciled herself to solitude. Again. And she wanted to laugh at his question; wanted to say, *That is all I am allowed to do in this place, is think about you and your family and their comfort and their guests and their ills.* She said, "Of course."

"I hate it here," he said. "You'd love Chicago. You ever been to Chicago?"

Anna shook her head. No sense in saying that she grew up in San Francisco. That she was not a stranger to city life.

"It is something to see. Particularly the buildings. They are impressive. Very beautiful. Some fairly new, the fire and all." He lay on his back across her bed. "Now there's something I'd like to do. Build."

Anna sat near him on the bed.

"My father has other plans," he finished.

"But you are rich. You can probably do whatever you want with your life." She moved closer. She wanted to feel control; she wanted to feel wealth by association.

He laughed. "Oh, yes, as long as it is acceptable to my parents. You know how parents are." He smoothed the hem of her skirt flat on the bed, superimposed it on *The Life Before.*

Anna shrugged her shoulders. "I was raised by my great-aunt Pauline. My mother died and I don't exactly recall her. They say I take after my father."

She could see the boy staring at her, examining each feature of her face and figure. She knew what he was thinking: that the skin was a rather light brown and the hair, while curly, was almost, well, *white* in construction. The mouth and nose were so beautiful; they belonged to the skin.

"Your father?" he said.

"Color seems to be a problem for some people."

"Yes," said the boy.

"Every day," she said, "I am aware of my color—made aware of my color or that I have a color or that I belong to a color. I am always my color first and Anna second. As if people can be divided, carved up that way." She stopped. "Ah, but you have your parents to contend with."

He pulled her over to him, pushed her shoulders down; Anna was willing. She had nothing to lose.

It was through this sad liaison that Anna came to be unemployed and left with a child to raise. She was angry with the boy and angry with herself. But not with Marianna, her baby; none of the bad feeling for the father bled through to her affection for the child.

When Anna learned she was pregnant, she left, much the same way she'd left the house in San Francisco. She did not tell the boy that she was having a baby; she kept it to herself. She did not want to hear him say that he loved her but could not marry her.

She simply left one day. "I'm leaving," she said, and by the next day was gone. Anna would not leave without telling her employers good-bye; that would be too much like running away and that she would not do. She does not run—they cannot make her—she *walks*.

So began the third phase of the four quarters that neatly separate Anna's life. As a housekeeper (*domestic* being the popular name in 1935) for the Rubens family, which included Mr. and Mrs. Rubens and their daughters, Glady Joe and Hy. Anna and Glady Joe were both seventeen.

For years, Mr. and Mrs. Rubens had had a steady stream of "wayward" girls employed in their home, living there, doing light housework, and cooking. They were sponsored by the Episcopal church and they stayed until the baby arrived, at which point the Rubenses bade farewell to the girl, as the girl did to her baby. It was understood that these infants were earmarked for adoption into responsible, barren families.

As Mrs. Rubens often said to friends who applauded her "good deeds": "It is the least we can do for a girl who finds herself in a bad way."

The pastor came to see Mrs. Rubens personally regarding the matter of Anna. "You see," he said, "this is a little more delicate than usual. Anna Neale is Negro." He did not add that she was as much Caucasian as she was Negro, because it simply would not have mattered; because this is the United States, with its archaic "one drop" rule, a legacy passed down from the Founding Fathers: *One drop of Negro blood makes one Negro.*

Mrs. Rubens said quickly, "Send her over. She is welcome here."

Anna almost felt worse working for a family that went out of its way to be "nice" to her, to include her, to be concerned about her pregnancy. To show interest in her condition, Anna knew, was altogether different from showing interest in *her.* She was more accustomed to the invisibility of her role at the ranch, or even the mrs.'s treatment of her. Pauline was now semiretired from her job there. It bothered Anna when the Rubenses insisted upon introducing her to their friends. She was embarrassed at Mrs. Rubens's calling her "our Anna" as in "You must meet our Anna." Mrs. Rubens took a special interest in Anna's diet ("Plenty of milk" and "You could stand to gain a little weight as well"). Mrs. Rubens let out old clothes of her own ("It's either you or

Goodwill, Anna"), and told Glady Joe and Hy "not to bother Anna."

Yet underneath it all, Anna could not quite shake off the chill, the tiniest hint of frost from Mrs. Rubens. Mr. Rubens was always polite to her, always asking her for things a housekeeper should provide, nothing more. He was often out of town on business and, in that respect, seemed more like an employer, making him more comfortable to be around.

In the evenings, when Anna had finished with her tasks, she frequently took nighttime walks, as she had on the ranch. Her center of gravity had shifted, making her stride less supple, a little more awkward, yet still carrying the same odd allure lusted after by the boy from Chicago. She would wander with her hand to her stomach, growing larger daily, her eyes scanning the sky. That was how she walked: hand to belly, eyes to heaven. As if she could somehow link the two. In the Philippines there is a Tagalog word *lehi*, as in "making *lehi*." Translated, it means that when a woman is pregnant, whatever obsesses her will manifest itself in the unborn child; so if one dreams of chicken beaks, one's child will be born with a chicken beak.

Anna was unaware of this as she moved in the shine of the moon, her palms resting on her stomach and her gaze cast upward. Perhaps making *lehi* is an instinctual reflex among women heavy with child. Or maybe she was simply crisscrossing it, unconsciously, with the tradition of wishing upon a star. Pauline had told her, *The sky belongs to nobody.*

The sky is free. Her unborn child, in this world, belonged to nobody.

You belong only to yourself.

When she came back one night, Glady Joe Rubens asked, "Where do you go at night, Anna?"

"Just walking," Anna said. "Nowhere special." Inside Anna had not forgotten the price paid earlier in her life for walking alone beneath the stars.

"I thought maybe I could go with you sometime."

No, no, she could not share her walks with anyone, certainly not another child of the family for which she worked. "Maybe," she said, vowing to herself that her nocturnal wanderings were now over for the duration of her stay in this house.

"I'd like that," said Glady Joe. "I truly would."

Anna suspected that, like Mrs. Rubens, Glady Joe wanted to show the world how charitable she could be to the "less fortunate." She did not stop to differentiate between what was genuine and what was false. What the difference between mother and daughter could be.

Anna quit her strolls, confined herself to her room after the dinner dishes were washed and put away. At first, she wrote letters to Pauline; sometimes she thought about getting in touch with the father of her baby, maybe just show up at his college back east. Really shock his parents.

The Rubenses provided her with an old radio that Anna felt might have belonged to the Rubenses' daughters, or the Flower Girls, as they were known around town. She was certain that it was donated at Mrs. Rubens's insistence. Oh, Anna could just hear her: "Now, Glady Joe, Hy, we have to be big enough to share with those who cannot get for themselves. You two can listen to the one downstairs." But there was so little on the radio that captivated Anna. There were the girlish, fey white singers who tried their hands at jazz or light blues, late at night, but often it did not sound right.

Anna began quilting. Pauline, who almost exclusively sewed and quilted for the mrs. by then, frequently sent her scraps, which Anna shoved into an old flour sack. Mostly the dark colors associated with the Amish quilts and some patterned pieces thrown in, maybe a true red or yellow. So heartbroken was the mrs. at the loss of *The Life Before* that she gave Pauline carte blanche to purchase yards of matching fabric (a luxury for the serious quilter) to fashion superior quilts. Anna's quilts cleverly joined scraps from Pauline's remnants. She made do with what came her way.

She began a crib quilt for her baby, using a traditional Amish pattern called *Broken Star.* Anna laid the back cloth and batting; she worked the tiny diamonds to create one huge star against a background of indigo.

One night, Glady Joe knocks softly on her door. Anna is momentarily startled; she often felt that once dinner was through and she retired to her room, she lived alone in this house. So separate from the Rubenses. "Anna?"

She sets her work aside, opens the door, and steps

back to let in Glady Joe. Glady Joe holds a book in her hand.

"Is this what you do?" Glady Joe fingers the hundreds of tiny diamond shapes. "I haven't seen you walking. That is, you must be quite fast because I don't see you leave." Glady Joe sits primly on the edge of the bed while Anna thinks, *Man, another white child of the house sittin' on my bed.*

"I haven't felt like walking."

"Oh."

Glady Joe shyly holds up her book. "I was wondering if you've ever read this?" Anna reads the title *Wuthering Heights* and shakes her head no.

"Would you like to borrow it? I mean, it reminds me of you—all that walking around—um, these people are always walking around, too. Across the moors. They spend a lot of time wandering." Glady Joe says, "I can't believe you are making this yourself. So many little pieces—how do you keep them all straight? And so striking. The colors, I mean."

"The women in my family quilt," says Anna, then, "Look, I'm pretty busy with this quilt. I want to finish it for my child"—she smiles briefly—"so I'm in a hurry."

Glady Joe rises. "I could leave the book. You could look at it when you have time."

"Don't bother," says Anna, then sees the hurt in Glady Joe's face. She feels guilty, then annoyed. Doesn't she have somewhere to go? Of course, she's not with Hy tonight because Hy is out with a group of friends. Anna heard her mention a special boy—Lee, Anna thinks—but her parents won't allow her to single-date; she's only fifteen. But Hy refuses to stay home; she is far more stylish and sociable than her sister. Glady Joe, too, seems "different" from most people in Grasse, but it is Hy who is more noticeable, with her tortoiseshell combs, sparkling dress clips worn with one of her mother's old sweaters, her embroidered school socks. New hairstyles copied from magazines published in New York and all her talk about Paris and Berlin and artists and such.

The Flower Girls often seem like outsiders when compared to the residents of Grasse; *Glady Joe more than Hy, but neither as much as me,* thinks Anna. Then Glady Joe is gone from her room and Anna is back at her *Broken Star.*

Later, as Anna heads down the hall to the bathroom, she hears Mrs. Rubens saying, "Sweetie, leave Anna alone. You two are very different people and you are old enough to understand what I mean by that."

Glady Joe protests. "Mother."

But Mrs. Rubens will allow no disharmony in her house. "It isn't fair to Anna or to you to start this thing up. These are not *my* rules; this is the way things are."

Anna pauses in the hallway. Not fair to Anna? Who is she to say what is fair and what is not? Goddamn these white folks anyhow. They think they know goddamn everything about everyone. Who said Anna was willing to be Glady Joe's friend, in any case? Though, she has to admit, company her own age would, at times, be a welcome thing.

Anna closes the bathroom door, strips off her

dress, shoes, and socks. She stares at herself in the mirror, which only reveals her body from the waist up (the waist that is rapidly disappearing), is dismayed by the heavy fullness of her breasts, which have finally lost that irritating tenderness (when the lightest brush of fabric across her nipples made her crazy). Her abdomen pooches, her hips have widened, and suddenly she is glad she has no man to see her naked. She is sad, too. There is no one to hold her, and she wonders if that is what drew her to the boy on the ranch in the first place—the longing to be held. She curses him for making her recall how much she likes being touched (no one had laid a hand on her since she left Pauline's). Anna believes that people can live without any number of pleasurable sensations, providing they never come into contact with them again. Because once they are reintroduced into a person's life, the need for that thing becomes consuming and uncontrollable.

She steps into the bath. As she lies on her back, her stomach and breasts peak out of the steaming water, like a small group of South Sea atolls. What had she expected from the boy? Love? Money? Social status? Affection? Revenge? A slap at the parents? At herself? She lifts the washcloth from the water and wrings it dry, the drops of water falling on her many-island body like a tropical rain. She imagines her baby floating in her womb as she floats in the tub and notes that it is asleep.

Wuthering Heights sits unopened on Anna's dresser, as Anna herself sits in the light of the bed-table lamp, eyes close to the work, stitching patches of

Broken Star. She is convinced that she hears someone on the other side of her door, silence, then
faint, disappearing footsteps.

Good, she thinks.

Until the next night, when Glady Joe comes
again to the door, asks to be let in. Anna leans back
in her chair, legs pushed slightly apart by her girth,
her lap containing the unfinished quilt. "Anna,"
says Glady Joe, "I thought I'd come by and see if
you'd like some ice cream. Mom made it. Tin
Roof Sundae."

"That does sound good," answers Anna.

In the kitchen, Mr. Rubens is telling some story
about a man in his office, someone who works for
him, as Mrs. Rubens listens raptly, clucking her
tongue in disapproval or surprise at all the appropriate moments. Says things like, "Some people just
never appreciate anything" or "They think the
world owes them a living." Maybe she'll glance in
Anna's direction and smile at her. Anna pretends to
be absorbed in her ice cream and wishes that she
could politely take it back to her room.

"So I said to him," says Mr. Rubens, jabbing the
air with his spoon, " 'There's a depression out there.
I don't need to tell you.' "

"Dear," agrees Mrs. Rubens, "you can only do
what is right. You can't do anything about anyone
else; no matter how much you may want to. Nothing goes unseen. We all have to live with ourselves.
Finally, I mean. In the end." She places a tiny bit of
ice cream on the tip of her spoon, takes it between
her lips.

"Of course, you are right" (Mrs. Rubens nods),

he says. "It's just that it sometimes makes you want to stop helping people—leave them to sink or swim, then let them see how good they had it."

"Of course," says Mrs. Rubens.

In comes Hy with two boys and a girl. ("Hello, Lee," says Mrs. Rubens, smiling. Lee says, "Evening, ma'am. Sir." Anna can see delight in Mrs. Rubens's shining eyes as she notes Lee's wonderful manners and fine demeanor. "The mark of being well bred," she says later.) The other boy is called James Dodd and the girl, Corrina something—Anna doesn't catch it.

"Lee brought me home," says Hy, curls loose after an evening out. Her dress is still nicely pressed—a burnt orange of that new, experimental fabric that is supposed to be so durable—and an elegant alligator belt, really too sophisticated for the young girl who wears it. Hy flings herself into a chair and exclaims, "Ooh, ice cream," offers some to her friends, who decline ("I promised to have Corrina home by ten-thirty"). Hy merely waves from the table, spooning ice cream into her mouth—a breach of etiquette that does not go unreprimanded by Mrs. Rubens ("Hy, we may live in Grasse but we still have manners"). But Hy just listens, eagerly awaiting the second helping of the ice cream that her mother is scooping into her bowl, never taking her eyes from the spoon to the bowl, with all the intensity of a cat being fed. With one elbow on the table, she slides off her earrings, one, then the other, tosses them toward her mother, thanking her for allowing her to borrow them.

"Well, they looked so pretty on you," says Mrs. Rubens.

Glady Joe asks, "Who do you like better—Lee or James?" and Hy answers, "Anyone who doesn't plan to be a farmer."

Anna is struck by nothing so much as the sense that she truly does not belong here, in this kitchen with Mr. Rubens chatting about the office and Mrs. Rubens's unconditional sympathy; the loaning of the earrings and the sisterly question about which boy makes the better date/prospect; and how she, Anna, completes the picture of American family perfection by being the charity, the evidence of the goodness of spirit that lives in this house, in this rural town, in the mid-1930s. She feels as if she is in a darkened theater watching something called The American Family, expecting a deep, resonant, informed voice-over to describe its habits, joys, ambitions, frustrations, and sorrows. Its desirability.

I am no part of this, thinks Anna. *Not only this house, but this world. This society.* This does not surprise her—what surprises her is the way in which she is both drawn to and repelled by what she sees. She is too late for dating; she would be happy to have a man of her own who kisses her when he comes in at night, calls her honey as he runs his strong, capable hands across her stomach, says good-evening to their baby inside her. They'll talk about their respective days; as tired as he is from working he'll gaze at her and say *my pretty girl.* Of course, there is a fantasy in itself—that he would be employed—a dream for half of America. She is lucky to be working, eating this ice cream, which makes it suddenly distasteful to her.

As she takes her bowl to the sink ("More dishes," she sighs), Glady Joe asks her if she'd like some more; after all, she is eating for two. Anna shakes her head; she wants to return to her room, lose herself in the *Broken Star*, and forget about being seventeen, unwed, unloved, pregnant, and outside the mainstream.

Glady Joe continues to come to Anna's closed door, usually bearing tea or something to show her or give her, while Anna accepts whatever is offered without much commitment. Each time, Glady Joe marvels over the progress of the quilt—its near completion; its complicated beauty. She asks more technical questions and Anna finds herself warming to the telling of how to make a quilt.

She relents, asks about the book that Glady Joe gave her. As Glady Joe begins to tell her the story of *Wuthering Heights*, she finds herself reading passages aloud; then beginning at the beginning. In the room there is only the sound of Glady Joe's voice reading—as Anna quilts—as Cathy and Heathcliff traverse the wild, desolate English landscape.

Anna likes this tale very much. She likes the remoteness of the setting, the drama of the friendship between the two and the way in which it continues and twists into the next generation. She loves the sense of Heathcliff and Cathy as outlaws; yet Cathy can function within society, while Heathcliff is destroyed and embittered by it. Anna likes his midnight soul; his dark heart.

She may stop quilting, ask Glady Joe to reread a passage, then repeat a section of it to herself; or she may ask questions or comment on what is being read. Sometimes Glady Joe sets the book in her lap, asks Anna what she thinks this or that means, the way in which it belongs in the story.

After *Wuthering Heights* comes *Jane Eyre*, the "natural extension," says Glady Joe, cracking open the novel. Anna is taken with the character of Jane: plain, honorable, smart, naïve Jane. She loves her backbone and is drawn to her in an altogether different way than she was to Heathcliff; she loves his badness as much as she loves Jane's goodness. Glady Joe and Anna disagree about the ending, as well as the reason behind Jane's affection for Mr. Rochester.

"It is because he is so great," sighs Glady Joe.

"It is because she is a domestic and lonely," corrects Anna.

Next comes *Pride and Prejudice*, which Anna does not care for ("Just like white folks," she thinks) and *Daisy Miller*, until Anna places her work in her lap one night and says, "Can't we get away from those English?" Everything has gone downhill since the Brontës. Glady Joe seems hurt that Anna is not warming to the same books that she does and says, "Henry James is American, not English."

"Same thing," says Anna.

Glady Joe tries *Madame Bovary* ("No," says Anna); then *Anna Karenina* ("No," says Anna). Then Pauline sends Anna a handwritten copy of a story called "Spunk" by Zora Neale Hurston.

Neale like me, thinks Anna.

Pauline's accompanying note reads: *I read this in someone else's magazine but I wanted you to have it so I copied it for you.* The shape and style of Pauline's handwriting causes Anna's throat to close and eyes to smart with tears.

And it is this story Anna reads to Glady Joe one night as she sits working on her first sample patch. Who says at the end, "I wonder who killed Spunk."

Anna says, "Now that's a story." She recognizes something that has been lacking in the continuing stream of stories and novels that Glady Joe has been reading to her. Pauline, now retired, regularly mails stories and poems to Anna, since she is in San Francisco with access to publications featuring black writers. Anna feels like a bridge between the literature of Glady Joe and Pauline: one sending her tales of her mother's culture, the other reading stories of her father's culture.

When Anna has a story to read, Glady Joe works her quilting sampler and listens. When Glady Joe reads, Anna works her own quilts. It is not long before Glady Joe tentatively tries her hand at Anna's quilts, placing the backing to the top piece, rescuing Anna from the tedium of the work.

Mrs. Rubens says something to Anna regarding adoption.

"But I'm not sending him out. I'm bringing him up myself," Anna says.

Mrs. Rubens acts as if she has received a shock with a hot wire. She blurts out, "Oh, but you can't!"

"Yes," Anna tells her, "I can and I will."

"But, Anna," says Mrs. Rubens, awkwardly fumbling for Anna's hand, "don't you want what is best for him? Don't you want him to have a good life?"

Anna wants to say, *What are you going on about? My child will still be called Negro and unless everything in this country changes before next week, my baby will have a rare chance at a "good life"; he will only have a "Negro life," which is made so hard even in the best of circumstances. Besides which, I am what is best for him.*

But she only says, "I'll do that. I'll give him what I can." She says this like she isn't scared, like she isn't seventeen and soon to be unemployed.

Glady Joe has begun seeing Arthur Cleary, a college boy, not from Grasse. It was actually Hy who brought him home first, with her coterie of friends, but it was Glady Joe who held his interest. Even a blind man could see that, Anna notes.

When Anna is taken to the hospital to deliver her baby, she finds herself in a segregated ward. Actually, it is a Not White ward, as Anna calls it, since she is sharing a large room with two women of Latin descent and another who looks to be Chinese, maybe part black. Anna is part white, but obviously not the right part, as she likes to say. The staff warms to her because she is so young and pretty, with her perfect brown skin, full mouth, the smart line of her nose, strength of her jaw, balance of her eyes.

Even the mrs. in San Francisco and the people on the ranch used to say, *She's colored but not truly colored, if you know what I mean* (whispering this last part). Perhaps her employers were nice to her because her features carried the vague underscoring of their own racial features; without awareness, responding "favorably" to them. Not that they want to claim her, thinks Anna, this part of her over which she has no control and is constantly judged.

Anna wonders if this is what the father of her baby made love to: the mix of her blood. Was he drawn to her kindred to him or to the contrast she posed?—for surely she embodied both in equal measure. She kisses Marianna's bald head.

Glady Joe and Hy come to see Marianna, though Hy fidgets so you can see that she'd rather be somewhere else, her bright smile not fooling Anna, and the sharpness of Glady Joe's voice when she speaks to her sister giving her away as well.

"Mom sends her best," says Hy, moving the blanket aside to get a good look at Marianna, hidden there in the circle of Anna's arm.

"Thank her for me," says Anna, not looking up. Marianna's eyes do not focus and she seems to flinch at the passing of a hand high above her eyes, or delight in the white uniform of the nurse as she leans across the child to take Anna's temperature.

"How do you feel? When do you go home?" asks Glady Joe.

"A couple of days. I got some ladies coming to

see me from the church." *Adoption ladies.* She does not say this, because she is not going to let them take her baby. (Mrs. Rubens alluded to the "shame" of raising a child without a father, while Anna wanted to scream that she could not be made to feel any more ashamed than the townspeople have already made her feel at being seventeen, unmarried, and pregnant. Been treated that way for so long that she had grown accustomed to it and it hardly touched her now.)

"Oh," says Glady Joe.

"Where will you go?" asks Hy.

"I'll find a room and a job."

"Maybe Mom—" says Hy, turning to Glady Joe, who gives her a look. Hy's voice drifts off. "Maybe not."

"Don't think about it," says Anna, gently rocking Marianna in her arms, heavy-lidded and tired.

Glady Joe looks down. "Whatever is best," she says, then, "I brought you something. A pamphlet I got from Arthur, who got it from someone else; anyway, it's called *Renaissance* and it has some stories I think you'll like." Anna takes it, recognizes it as a booklet already sent to her by Pauline. It is writing by black Americans in New York. But she is moved by the thought.

"Thank you," she says.

Anna gets a job working as a bookkeeper for the local five-and-dime. At first, she enjoys the challenge of balancing the figures, ordering the day's take in a general ledger. But soon it becomes rote, a task she could perform in her sleep. It doesn't even pay that well, and she is cooped up in an air-less, windowless back office without company. It occurs to her that what she does is not unlike housework; that is, she repeats the same tasks day in, day out, the figures unbalanced yet properly totaled by the end of the day. Even though there may be a variety of things to do, they are always the same each week ("Make the beds on Monday, laundry on Tuesday, the floors on Wednesday, dusting on Thursday, and so on"). Debits and credits. Balance. Housework. And sitting all day is as bad as being on your feet, she discovers. Since she is the only black person here, she is virtually friendless. Sometimes she wonders if this job was given to her as a favor to someone else.

But then there is Glady Joe, who occasionally stops off for a visit. Or comes by the room Anna rents to play with Marianna. And who is seeing a great deal of Arthur Cleary, fueling the rumor that they are, in fact, engaged.

When Glady Joe was expecting the twins, Francie and Kayo, she asked Arthur to hire Anna to help her. So there was Anna, standing at the Clearys' front door, holding three-year-old Marianna by her soft, fat hand, again living under the same roof as Glady Joe.

If Anna was attractive, then Marianna was strik-ing, embodying the graceful movements of her mother, the same full mouth; her father's hazel eyes; her skin neither as dark as her mother's nor as light as her father's; her hair softer, more relaxed; her fa-ther's hands; her mother's pretty smile; her mother's figure, only stretched a little taller, but Anna just the same.

Even when she was a child, Marianna's beauty made people stop on the street. The usual look for the citizens of Grasse is white, heavy, pliable, gone to early middle age before thirty. The women married so young, worked so diligently beside equally hardworking (sometimes, difficult) husbands, with housework to do, meals to prepare, children to raise, that they let themselves go until the effort it would require to reclaim their lost looks seemed insurmountable. But even on their best days in their younger years, they would fade away beside the beauteous Marianna, rich, smooth child of Anna, maid to Arthur and Glady Joe Cleary.

Again Anna became the ghostly witness to the American Dream; not much changed from the Rubenses', though Glady Joe explained early on, "This is not my mother's house." Anna nodded, wanted to finish the wash already so she could get Marianna to bed and work on her newest quilt. It was another for Marianna, made of shoe appliqués in all styles, sizes, and colors. Glady Joe preferred it to the *Broken Star*, which was a traditional pattern. The shoe quilt was pure Anna.

Next came *Forest Leaves*, with its green-and-brown accents, a tall tree at one side, the rest of the quilt filled with wild, kicked-up swirling leaves. This, too, for Marianna.

Now Anna makes a quilt for herself of invented constellations pressed against a field of deep blue. Polaris dominates the design. Glady Joe still occa-

sionally reads to Anna, but now it is in the afternoon, when Francie and Kayo are down for their
naps and Arthur is at the office. Her evenings are
filled with Arthur these days, and the twins, too, require her attention. Anna and Glady Joe read and
quilt in the sun room so Anna can watch Marianna
playing in the garden, watch her as she roots around
in the dirt ("Don't touch," commands Anna; "be
gentle with the flowers," and Marianna looks up at
her mother, eyes trying to puzzle out what she is
being told, testing to see if it is good advice to follow), patting the earth around the base of the plants,
mud beneath her fingernails, tasting the mud on her
tongue. Tasting the grass and lifting an earthworm
pinched in her filthy fingers, only to drop it quickly
(as if it were aflame), vigorously rubbing her hand
on the front of her dress in revulsion. But Anna can
see that Marianna derives odd pleasure from the
taste of the mud.

Anna longs for a man of her own with whom
to have another child. Someone for Marianna to
grow up with, to be kin to; Anna worries that Marianna will grow up, disconnected with the other
children around her, unable to find her kindred.
She appears occasionally bored, but not lonely,
Anna has to admit. Perhaps it is only Anna who
feels lonely.

Glady Joe becomes more adept at quilting and
seems to enjoy it. Actually seems a little sad when
Francie and Kayo cry from their cribs and quilt time
is past.

Glady Joe takes over more of the tedious grunt
work, freeing Anna to devote her energy to design

and detail. She grows more experimental: Showers of light fall from the sides of flying sailboats; flowers grow feet and walk about in hidden canyons; Miró-like abstracts fill vast fields of lavender, scarlet, and amber. Glady Joe does not seem to mind her part in the quilts. She is a fast learner.

They still read aloud: Hurston's *Drenched in Light* as well as other stories.

Two things happen: Glady Joe begins her circle with Anna as the unspoken leader and teacher; black Anna and white Glady Joe find equal footing. They become true friends because they share, complement each other; one does not solely take on the role of comforter or comforted; one does not exclusively receive while the other takes. Theirs is an exchange. Of course, Anna recognizes her status is changing in the country with the advent of civil rights, but she sees civil rights as a demand and a gift when it should be neither. Black Americans should not have to demand, plead, or cajole any more than white Americans should be in a position to withhold or bestow. And there is the "gratitude" issue; the one side wishing the other side would be grateful, when the other side cannot for the life of them figure out exactly *what* they should be grateful for. So here in this little town of Grasse, Anna achieves equality in her own way. Let anyone try to tell her otherwise or wrest it from her. Just let them.

Then came that nasty business when James Dodd was dying and Glady Joe nearly destroyed every fragile object in the house. Certainly, it was no secret to Anna, who kept the house (the same way she kept books at the five-and-dime), that Arthur and Glady Joe Cleary maintained separate bedrooms. ("Why, if I had a man of my own," mused Anna one afternoon, "I'd hold him close to me at all times, revel in his warm breath, thrill to his touch. We would exchange love; even if miles apart, we would exchange love. He would walk the world and still know that we belong to each other." Glady Joe did not look up from her embroidery. "Yes, one would think that, I suppose.")

There is the night, with James laid up in the hospital and Hy over to the house, when the three of them decide to watch slides. As Arthur sets up the slide projector, Anna hears, "Goddamn bulb." (To Glady Joe:) "Did you think to buy some extra?"

Hy swings by Anna, through the dining room and into the kitchen, to pour something to drink while Glady Joe searches for a good light bulb and Arthur tinkers with the projector.

"I know about you and Arthur," hisses Anna.

And Hy is not stupid enough to say something like *Whatever do you mean?* like some wronged, simpering belle. Instead she meets Anna's look head-on and says, "Actually, I don't believe you do."

"No one expects you to live an exemplary life, only a truthful one."

"Anna," says Hy, "I've known you most of my life and I love you like family but this is none of your business."

"I can see how you love your family," says Anna.

"*If* you were married," says Hy, "you'd understand. *If* your husband were dying."

"You mean I'd understand loss? About wanting something for yourself? For someone who has known me practically her entire life, I am surprised at how little *you* understand. Do you really think you are the only person ever told, No, you can't have this thing? The only one set aside by God?" Anna trembles. "Just don't love me like family. Will you do that for me?"

Glady Joe and Hy sit side by side on the sofa, with Arthur behind them working the projector and Anna secreted in the shadows of the dining room. Tonight they are searching out photographs of James, who lies in the hospital, close to death.

There is Hy on the screen, just after Will was born; he stares uninterestedly at his mother. Hy's attention is focused on Will, though James is by her side. She is wearing a sophisticated black suit with gold hoops in her pierced ears and a custom-made gold choker about her throat. Her hair is pulled back with a black velvet cord and her eyes are hidden behind cats'-eye sunglasses. James looks more like Grasse in his white dress shirt, jeans, and work boots. "God, look at us," says Hy, laughing. "I can't believe I dressed like that around here."

"Yes," says Glady Joe, "but you looked like somebody. You really did."

"And James," says Hy, "like he can't seem to

make up his mind as to being a farmer or a businessman. Poor James."

"Wait, wait," says Arthur, holding a slide close to the light before slipping it into the projector. "This one you'll remember." And suddenly all four of them are seated at a dime-sized table, at the Coconut Grove in Hollywood sometime in 1963. They are drinking martinis and sweet Manhattans, unaware these cocktails are out of vogue. Both Hy and Glady Joe, easily in their mid-forties, look ageless; they could be just that much younger or slightly older, each at a point where she has a certain glow or grace, which comes for the first time in a woman's life when she is very young, then visits a second, final time, in middle age.

Glady Joe's black dress is cut straight across her bosom with a jade-and-ruby broach affixed to one of the spaghetti straps. Her hair is done up in a French twist. Hy, on the other hand, glitters in green velvet with beading. Around her neck, again, is the gold choker, and in her ears antique emerald earrings—a gift from James for their wedding anniversary, which they are all celebrating this night. James's forearm lies across the table, his other arm rests on Hy's bare shoulder. He smiles for the camera, but one can imagine him turning all his attention back to his sparkling wife as soon as the shutter clicks. Glady Joe and Arthur are not touching, but smiling over at Hy and James, both looking in the same direction without crossing their lines of vision.

"God, that was fun," says Hy, "to be out of Grasse for the weekend."

"And remember the Ambassador?" asks Arthur.

"I remember," says Glady Joe, as she fights with the anger that wells up inside her, looking at this record of their lives, now made so false by her husband and sister. She does not want to give herself away. She sits quietly, as if she feels nothing.

More slides of Will as an infant/toddler/child/ teenager/college student. Slides of Gina. Of Francie and Kayo. Slides of Finn, Will's daughter by a girl named Sally, who believed in free love and no ties that bind. ("But you have a *baby*," insisted James when they announced they would not marry in any case. "What stronger tie is there in nature? Why not give her your name? Tell me that. Make me understand, Will." Hy winces at the memory of Will storming from the house with Sally and little Finn, saying, "Just kiss your granddaughter good-bye, *James.*" Which broke James's heart—to have his grandchild taken from him and to hear his own son call him "James," never again to call him Dad. And the way he spat out his father's name, with such naked disregard. Crazy to think that Will and Sally ended up married after all, only to divorce a short time later.)

Birthday parties with James dressed like Zorro; Christmas with Arthur decked out as Santa Claus ("Of course I'm not the *real* Santa Claus," he told Will and Gina and Francie and Kayo, who always spent Christmas Eve together; "I'm only one of his helpers").

Photographs of James's new office or Arthur's new building; pictures of investments like an oil well or a citrus grove.

There were Easter Bunny suits, Halloween face makeup when James took the kids out, leaving Hy at home to dole out candy to the trick-or-treaters. Anniversaries, birthdays, holiday meals. And the changing furniture of their respective houses, as Early American gave way to Danish Modern, which eventually made room for some low-slung Japanese items; the best of each era always remaining to be blended with the new arrivals. Always upscale; never looking back. Their houses eventually reflecting the many tastes and stages of their lives, the embarrassingly tacky juxtaposed with the refined.

Anna stands behind all of them as she watches the screen from the dining room. She sees herself serving cake or posing with Marianna in the garden. Marianna older than the other children by a good ten years. She looks solemn and smart and gorgeous. Anna shy to stand beside her.

Marianna's high school graduation goes up on the screen along with the celebration dinner at the Clearys' house; Marianna's excitement at being accepted to an agricultural college up north (not knowing immediately that her tuition was being paid by Anna and Glady Joe together).

Anna watches this summary of their lives, feeling just the smallest regret that she did not allow herself to be photographed more often—as if by hiding from the camera she could somehow deny just how inextricably bound her life was to the people in the pictures. *Why, there is no simple way to show either of our personal histories without including the other's.*

Mostly she thinks, *My Marianna was a beautiful*

child, and the pump of adoration into her heart almost feels as if it could knock her over. *My Marianna*.

Instructions No. 7

TAKE A VARIETY OF FABRICS: VELVET, SATIN, SILK, cotton, muslin, linen, tweed, men's shirting; mix with a variety of notions: buttons, lace, grosgrain, or thick silk ribbon lithographed with city scenes, bits of drapery, appliqués of flora and fauna, honeymoon cottages, and clouds. Puff them up with: down, kapok, soft cotton, foam, old stockings. Lay between the back cloth a large expanse of cotton batting; stitch it all together with silk thread, embroidery thread, nylon thread. The stitches must be small, consistent, and reflect a design of their own.

The inexperienced eye will be impressed by the use of color, design, appliqué, and pattern, but the quilter will hold the work between her fingers and examine the stitches. Or she will lay out the quilt and analyze the overall pattern the stitches follow. The quilting can resemble birds and flowers and hearts afire and fleurs de lys. It can look like anything. While the nonquilter will recognize the craftsmanship of this quilt, she will not be "consciously" aware of it; she will only sense that she is viewing a superior work and mistakenly attribute it to a clever use of fabric contrast and color.

Consider the fact that some roses cannot survive the environment into which they are born. Consider the fact that grafting a more delicate plant onto a hardier stock will probably make for a superior rosebush—one that can not only withstand the hostile environment, but thrive within it.

English walnut grafted to black walnut results in a less greasy nut meat. The sour orange used as a base for the Mars orange is virtually uneatable, while the fruit of the Mars is very sweet.

If the Brazilian nut will accept the soybean graft the product will be nutritionally superior, one rich in protein.

A budding knife resembles a fish-boning knife with its sharp blade and curved tip.

A seam ripper is a curve of sharp metal at the end of a long handle.

Here are your tools: A budding knife and a flat board with four wheels and gloves and thin white rubber bands. That is all. Your needs for the graft procedure are simple, unadorned, well defined. There is no question unanswered.

Except why would a rose germinate in unfriendly soil; why does it seek its life only to find it cannot survive it? Do not think about it now.

The almond trees of the San Joaquin Valley look like dark trunks attached to white bases. They are painted white. This is better to see them in the shadows of the grove and has nothing, really nothing, to do with grafting, though it would appear that it does. This demarcation of base root to upper trunk.

You understand these divisions, this fusion of two distinct elements.

People remark on your beauty. You want to say that you are a result of polarities of color and culture; that you are the gorgeous, restless sum of your parts; that you are what people are so afraid of, this rare sort of mix. But the aggregate that is you is so seamless, so smooth, that no one—including yourself—can see where your father's lines leave off and your mother's pick up.

T-bud grafting requires a T cut in the primary growth. This should be done on the side of the stalk, just below the node—or eye, as it is commonly called. Be sure the section to be grafted also contains an eye. All the information the rosebush needs is held in the eye. Now. Toward the base, where the plant meets the soil, slip the eye into the T. Your stalk should look "whole," not like two separate pieces; the fusion should give the illusion of oneness.

Take a piece of white rubber. Cut a hole in it. Wrap securely around the graft area (a bobby pin will hold it in place). This serves to keep out infection and dirt. Remember: The meeting of the eye to the primary growth must be clean and perfectly fitted. If you do not graft close enough to the base, where the plant meets the soil, it will dry up and the graft will be unsuccessful.

On the matter of a perfect match—this is really more important for tree grafts than for rosebush grafts, but you are a perfectionist by nature and would be loath to perform a sloppy joining in the first place.

Remember the names: primary growth and meristematic growth and the eye. The eye knows everything. The eye serves as biological memory. (Q: What has four eyes but cannot see? A: Mississippi.) Soon the graft will take and the rubber piece can be removed and discarded.

Grafted roses can be found by the side of municipal highways, in building lobbies, in nurseries, or in the hands of a lover, passed from one to the other.

Fusion, union, grafting, joining, sex, friendship, love: the difficult combination of disparate elements.

Virginia Law, 1753: A woman servant who begets a bastard child by her master shall be sold by the church wardens for one year after her time is expired. If a free Christian white woman has a child by a Negro or mulatto she shall pay the church warden 15 pounds current money or be sold by them for five years and the child made a servant until thirty-one years of age. Any intermarriage between black and white, free or bound, shall be fined 10 pounds and spend six months in jail without bail.

Virginia Law, 1910: Any person having one sixteenth or more of Negro blood shall be deemed a "coloured person."

Virginia Law, 1924: A white person must marry a white person and that any falsification of birth records regarding race (in order to marry) shall be deemed illegal and punished.

Virginia Law, 1932: Any intermarriage between

white and coloured is illegal and carries a sentence of between one and five years in a penitentiary.

Antebellum American South: Slaves cannot be manumitted except for special and specific circumstances; cannot be taught to read or write; cannot worship in private; cannot bear firearms; cannot purchase medicine; cannot marry, hence, cannot have "legitimate" children; cannot "own" their children or spouses if not free; cannot control their own points of sale; cannot break a will leaving them as inherited property to a named beneficiary; cannot gather in a group; cannot have relations with white persons, though the white persons may have relations with them; cannot testify in a court of law; cannot bear witness; *can* be "striped," linked in a coffle, owned, raped, disfigured, and murdered; cannot keep their own earnings when hired out to someone else; and, much later, cannot attend school, ride buses, frequent restaurants, or drink from anything marked WHITE ONLY.

Your favorite quilts are those that are abstract. You try to love the more representational styles of quilts, try to warm to the *Honeymoon Cottage* pattern, the *Drunkard's Progress*, or the *Repeating Fans*, but you cannot. You prefer the quilt that looks like music or dance; the ephemeral arts. You stitch a flurry of magenta and blue crescents and you know *exactly* what you are seeing; you know what they represent. These abstractions look like pictures to you, even if they do not to the other quilters in the circle. They accuse you of rejecting tradition. You counter by saying that you are making your own traditions, that they are correct—*tradition* has little meaning for you.

And you, born in 1935, in college in 1953, feel both affection and disgust for this place in which you were born, this hostile soil. Because nothing has really changed in your lifetime; because you carry more than one sixteenth Negro blood; because you understand the theory and application of separate but equal; because your daily and biological life is so tightly wound into a world that appears to want to forget you exist; because you cannot travel freely in the United States; because you are seen as black; because Rosa Parks has not yet made her famous bus ride; because of all this, because you are educated and black and white and not welcome in this place of your birth; because you understand, historically, where you stand, you will leave this place.

You will relocate elsewhere, to make you strong.

You will one day return and make quilts like your mother before you and her mother before her, and all of the women will be suitably impressed at the expert way in which you join your pieces of cloth. They will think your mother taught you well.

Grafting Roses

MARIANNA HAS MORE LOVERS THAN SHE IS AWARE OF; that is, she is admired from afar. These admirers court her in secret, in the safety of their dreams. When they see her sitting in a café or walking to her job at the nursery or buying bread for dinner, they think, *In my dreams we are together,* then they return home to their wives and children and girlfriends. It is harmless; they would never think to force themselves on her; she is simply a passing fancy. Because she is so exotic in her looks, as well as being an expatriate, as well as being a woman working at a man's job, where virtually no women work. Because it is difficult to discern her heritage at a quick glance. Because she walks with the grace of her mother, Anna Neale, who is back home in Grasse, United States.

What her admirers do not, cannot, know, is that even her "real" lovers cannot truly have her, cannot claim her for their own exclusively. This leaves them unhappy and confused.

For Marianna, the wedding vow is as binding as

the deathbed promise. Her lovers do not know this about her either.

By the time Marianna went to college, Anna was living outside the Clearys' house, coming back only to cook supper occasionally for Glady Joe and Hy. Anna also arrived, once a week, to lead the Grasse Quilting Circle, which had begun at Glady Joe's house. Anna now made enough money to live by making and selling quilt patterns in town. She told her customers (some of whom came across great distances), "Yes, you could send away for a pattern, but mine are better because they are specialized. Not a factory item." And that was Anna's gift; that she could meet with a woman and translate her story onto tissue paper, which was then used as a pattern for a custom quilt. Anna could always come to understand at least one important element in the character of her customer—perhaps not understand the entire woman, but, then, quilters work in patches and bits.

Sometimes, if a particularly nasty woman came to her, Anna represented her personality as an extreme opposite; if the woman was a bitch, Anna fashioned her pattern as if she were a saint. Imagine what her friends thought as the woman proudly displayed her quilt, saying, "And this is me." The viewer looking from quilt to woman back to quilt, wondering how someone could be so blind to themselves, could possibly be flattered by such a subtle insult.

Anna never lost her edges; never truly yielded. Marianna inherited her internalized strength, the way in which she kept her own secrets. It was not easy to be close to Anna or Marianna.

Marianna told herself, *I will never keep house for anyone.* It was by luck and talent that Anna had parlayed her association with Glady Joe into a business and quilting circle.

"Why do you continue to cook for those people?" asked Marianna.

"Because I'm very good," Anna told her.

"I don't see how you can do it. Not that it isn't honest work, but you have your own things now. Things that belong to you."

"This is true," said Anna, "but Glady Joe and I go back. I don't have to tell you. And the money helps out."

"I can give you money," said Marianna.

"Maybe I want my own," said Anna.

Marianna grew up and went to an agricultural college in northern California, with every intention of returning to Grasse (Bakersfield is the "Bread Basket of the World"). But when she graduated in 1953, there was not a farmer in Kern County who would hire her. "A woman?" they said. "A Negro woman? Not in this life." Sometimes they laughed or ignored her or called her honey.

No one ever suggested to Marianna that she "understand" the men's perspective. No one ever said, Look, it's their ignorance. Anna told her, "Don't listen to that trash," and Marianna was not raised to "listen" in any case. Not by a mother with distinguished quilting skills and her own business.

Sometimes people said, "How extraordinary that Marianna wants to work in agriculture, out in the fields with the farmers."

"Why extraordinary?" asked Anna. "Because she's a woman? Because she's black?"

And the people would shrug their shoulders and say, "Well, both."

So Marianna ended up tending roses in the south of France, fairly close to a town called Grasse ("I like the symmetry of it," she laughed), for a company that supplied flowers to much of Europe.

Cut roses and miniature roses grow in a greenhouse. Garden roses and roses to be planted along the highway are grown outside. Marianna lies on a flat board with wheels, slowly rolling up and down the furrows, grafting roses—lying on her stomach to save her back.

Marianna remembers being told that she will know she is in love because she will feel elation in his presence. Or perhaps it was something that she read. In any case, that is her definition of love: elation in one another's presence. She likes that idea; waits to experience it.

After five years in France, Marianna finds herself living with one man and having a warm love affair with another. At night she comes home to Alec, who, like herself, is an American. He rubs her shoulders, which are strong and defined from the years of grafting; he traces his tongue along the small of her tired back. Alec never fails to make her heart quicken. He reads to her late at night, in bed, sometimes after sex, allowing her the luxury of drifting off to the sound of his wondrous voice. Occasionally, they argue, exchange unforgivable, angry words, but this is rare; they recover. That is, it does not undermine them.

Alec and Marianna live outside Antibes. The house is like an accidental structure in the center of a turbulent garden of flowers and grass. It quite takes Marianna's breath away, the uncivilized landscape, with its scents and varieties of color and form. The weathered brick house has an enormous wraparound porch, but it all looks to be on its way to being an abandoned dwelling, the garden soon to reclaim the land.

The first day they lived there, Alec came into the garden carrying two bottles of red wine. "Italian," he said of the wine, then dropped to his knees in the tall, unkempt grass and began working the cork with the corkscrew.

Marianna felt awkward standing as this man struggled at her feet, and she soon sat down beside him, feeling unexpected pleasure at the heat of the early evening and the caress of the dry grass on her bare legs. "I could grow to like this," she said, smiling at Alec.

"It is like heaven," he agreed, passing her the open bottle, watching her take a long swallow of wine. Her throat smoothly arched, eyes closed.

For the first time in her life, Marianna knew the luxury of love. She basked in Alec's affection and grew more beautiful as a result. She was convinced that this was what she had always been waiting for and saw her life sharply divided between her life before Alec and her life since knowing Alec. She wondered how it was that her mother could live her life without someone to adore her and to be adored.

Then Marianna met Noe, who was nothing like Alec, but to whom she felt drawn in any case. He was transferred to her section and she knew him only casually at first. They talked about work, about gardening, about France and America. They argued different points; Noe sometimes hurting her with his violent perspective on things. They would eat lunch together on the ugly wood benches behind the main greenhouse or he brought lunch and drove them both down to the ocean, where they sat close to each other on the seawall, lamenting the idea of having to return to the nursery to finish the work day. Their conversations unobtrusively moved from the general topics of work and politics, and pressed into the personal; Marianna noticing and not noticing this quiet shift; Marianna both startled and charmed.

She told herself that she loved Alec, could love only one man at a time; loved Alec because he was good to her and, besides, they were both Americans, giving them a deeper understanding of each other. But Alec was white, too.

Noe, on the other hand, was black, understood that about her, but he was also French, and had numerous misguided notions about the United States to which he vigorously and emphatically held, regardless of what she said.

Noe brushed her loosely curled hair ("Your father's side, I guess?" he said, having seen a photograph of Anna), lifted it above her neck, laid kisses on the line of her spine. He said to her, "Leave your lover and live with me," as they dressed in the afternoon, having skipped lunch, choosing to spend their time in his flat.

Marianna did not know what to say, so she said nothing. Pretended that he had not spoken to her at all. She was wrestling with this new discovery about herself: that she could still deeply love Alec while feeling desire for Noe. Did she love Noe? This made her ill, this involvement with two men; it wrenched what she had with Alec, confused what she felt for Noe; told herself what she had thought was the Real Thing never was, that nothing was real.

She became irritable at home. Critical and restless. When Alec tried to touch her she would swat his hand away saying, "Leave me alone. Stop crowding me all the time."

Marianna noticed every annoying thing Alec did, things a lover would never see, and as she rode her belly board up and down the furrows at work, she found herself thinking about leaving Alec. She thought about breaking it off with Noe. As she lay prone, wrapping the white rubber around the stem, protecting the newly joined split from infection, she discovered that she was in the untenable position of loving two men when she had previously thought she could love only one.

In the midst of her tumultuous love life, Marianna considered returning home. It was becoming more difficult for people to determine her background. She knew she could "pass" if she so desired, that she could be taken for white and not black; she resembled her father as well as her mother, though she had inherited Anna's cool walking grace and her kinship with the moon.

But she refused to deny her African-American heritage, for to do so would deny Anna, and that she would not do; act as if her mother had never existed! She considered Anna's blood the proudest part of herself, not something to be falsified. It would betray that languorous walk.

It was so odd, really, this anglicizing of her features as her face matured, as if her white history would not be ignored, either, and her body was some sort of quiet battleground, with her father's side slowly but surely assuming more and more territory. It was frightening to see in herself the man she never knew; become someone she did not know. Marianna began to feel the most profound need to be back with her mother. To steady herself.

Alec learned of her sexual betrayal.

Marianna says, "It isn't technically betrayal," as they sit across the kitchen table from each other that night, "if no promises are made. We are not married. I did not promise to be sexually exclusive and I did not ask it of you." She knows their agreement has been implicit; she knows she is killing him.

"But I *was*." His eyes well up with tears that do not fall. To which she repeats, "I did not ask it."

She takes a deep breath, hating the sound of her

own voice. "I don't believe in monogamy. In my love, I have always been true to you. Always."

"I want to marry you," he says miserably, not looking at her.

"I'll still love you," she tells him.

"What the hell does that mean?" He wipes his nose with a swipe of his hand. "If you don't want me, then you could love me or hate me—the result would be the same."

"Did I say I didn't want you?" she demands.

"Yes," he tells her, "that is exactly what you said."

She is silent, thinking, *I am losing him and I cannot lose him.* Yet she cannot stop thinking about or wanting Noe, who lies in his flat across town, wanting, she knows, to hear from her. There is no resolution. Everything in her life is at war with everything else: her mixed blood; her Americanism transplanted into French soil; her attraction to catastrophic love (she can love more than one person at a time); being a woman working a man's job. She cannot be made whole, cannot be joined together with herself—or with someone else.

"Can we just go to sleep?" she asks.

In bed, Alec cannot touch her; he turns his back to her, cocooned in the covers. Once, during the night, his arm strikes out and hits her, but when she sits up in bed to scream at him, she discovers that he is fast asleep. This makes her cry, knowing that he could not slap her in his waking life but would hurt her in his dreams.

Marianna packed her valise, told Alec she was leaving. Alec begged her to stay, told her that she would get over this other man, that he would be patient, help her as long as she gave them another chance. But Marianna shook her head. No, it could not be done. Because she had been longing for Noe, aching for him, and thought it was Noe whom she loved better. Loved more. Alec kicked the door shut behind her.

She stayed with Noe a week, only to discover that she still loved Alec, missed his kisses in the small of her tired back. That she felt emptied out. Noe accused her of being unable to love a black man.

"Funny," she said. "Alec said I was leaving because he was white."

But Noe did not kick the door shut behind her. He gathered her in his arms, held her so tightly Marianna thought he would break her, then, without kissing her, wished her luck. They even made a date for lunch that Marianna knew they would not keep, simply because there was no reason to.

After Alec and Noe came Jacques, then Giles, then Michel, then Benjamin, then Luciano. Again and again, Marianna fell in love, had affairs, then moved on with her life. There was something in her that spurned marriage; she did not know what it was. All she knew was that she was capable—no, destined—to love more than one man at a time, and that this could hardly be good for a marriage.

Sometimes the men she spent time with treated her badly because she refused to marry them. It was not simply her refusing to marry them as much as she would say, "I just don't want to marry anyone."

They would look at her with hurt, angry eyes (Jacques, Giles, Michel, Benjamin, and Luciano) and ask, "I could be 'anyone' to you?"

All the while, Alec continued writing her letters, which she seldom answered. His last letter said, *This makes the third letter I have sent without a reply. Don't make me beg.*

Marianna eventually gave up on lovers altogether. She decided that she was too cold a woman to be a mistress and too stubborn to be a wife. She wanted things her way, and compromise held no charm for her; Marianna of the divided heart and soul.

She felt ready to go home. Anna had written her about the changes for the black man: There was Dr. King's message of love and Malcolm X's to use whatever means were necessary and its implication of force. He said, If you don't answer Dr. King's knock at your door, you'll have to answer mine. There was President Johnson's Great Society; marches and protests and violence and rage and the unmourned death of Jim Crow (*At last,* wrote Anna). And still this was not quite enough to lure her home.

What brought her back was missing her mother and the way her garnet necklace caught and re-fracted the light. And Marianna felt older, stronger, for her stay in France, which was not devoid of prejudice, but it took a different form.

She was done with grafting; she had grown tired of it. No matter how well she did it, it would always have to be done again to new plants. The roses simply could not be bred to stand alone; they would always require the hardier base. The fusion of the bushes can only give the illusion of oneness, but can never truly be one. Finally, when she recalled her many love affairs, she became convinced that they indicated a cold heart, one that will not allow closeness or for anyone to be close. This astonishes her, because she used to think that her many lovers were the sign of a great capacity to love, a capacity greater than any one of her lovers could match. Now she knows that it was an inability to love.

She said good-bye only to Alec, who seemed happy to see her arrive at the house and disappointed that she had come just to say farewell.

"Not Kern County, Marianna," he said. "Don't go back to Grasse. Go to San Francisco or New York. That's where you should be."

But she told him, "Grasse is my home. Let those who don't like me move out. You know I dislike making adjustments for anyone."

He smiled. "Yes," he said, "I know that about you."

When Marianna arrived back in California, she discovered Constance's rose garden. Constance would nod to Marianna as she passed by, Marianna occasionally pausing to dispense advice on pruning or soil or disposing of aphids. Constance knew that Marianna was Anna's daughter, recently returned from France. She remembered Anna mentioning her, showing her picture to the quilting circle. There was Marianna, sitting in a neglected garden of some friend's house, drinking wine, barefoot in the tall grass. *She's lovely,* thought Constance.

Anna said, "Constance, my girl is about your age, give or take a year." Which made Constance realize that the photograph of the girl in the grass was rather dated.

And Marianna recalled her mother writing about some woman who had "fine roses you should see."

Still, the two women did not converse freely when Marianna happened by.

Constance had to travel back east to see her family. She was not sure how long she would be gone, so she asked Glady Joe to look after her roses. The first day Glady Joe went to Constance's, she stopped by Anna's to ask Marianna to join her (Marianna, who had been tending Glady Joe's garden since her return). When Constance arrived home it was Marianna she had to thank for the healthy state of her roses. After that, when Marianna had time, she would visit Constance, working the flowers by her side, usually in comfortable silence.

Marianna was sometimes asked—Marianna, who is now on the late edge of middle age—"How can you, an educated woman, work for a white lady, caring for her garden?" Often, it was a white person who posed this question.

Marianna knew that pride and self-worth were everything and that there was not a farmer in Kern County that she would consider working for today, in 1988, and that maybe her life had been stacked against her, but Glady Joe's garden was the most beautiful sight for miles around.

No one ever said to her, "Marianna, Grasse is an ugly, dusty place—how is it you can perform such

miracles in Glady Joe's garden?" For this bit of land
was Marianna's small miracle, her contribution to
beauty in this hot, colorless place.

Anna resolved her life (as much as a life can be
resolved, which is not saying much at times) and
became more content, a little calmer and accepting.
She was well aware of what her life was not, would
never be, and she was angry over Marianna's life,
but she could not bear the weight of that feeling
anymore. Though her quilting business allowed her
artistic expression, a living, and respect, she still
could not forget her early love of the heavens, and
cursed and blessed her youth. What could have
been. Still.

In turn, Marianna took on the tolerance of her
mother. She joined the quilting circle at Constance's
insistence ("Because you are my friend," said Constance, knowing that Marianna could not possibly
know how unusual that was for Constance to have
a woman friend). Marianna liked Constance's un-
ruffled independence, so unlike the other women in
the circle. She had a hard time imagining Constance
as a married woman—it did not seem possible—
even though she had slightly known Howell Saunders. Of course, she and Constance were the same
age. About Dean, Marianna laughs to herself; no,
she would not pass judgment on Constance and
Dean—not with what she knows of love.

Marianna is drawn to abstract quilts—seemingly
random splashes of color and texture, with strange,
unlikely composition. They express what she has to
say.

* * *

Anna and Marianna are stuck, being both black and white; being neither black nor white; and while they do not particularly like white people, they eventually grow to accept Glady Joe, Constance, and the memory of the boy from Chicago. One could say they appear more comfortable with their difficult beauty.

The quilters accepted Anna and Marianna, and no one ever made the mistake of saying, "We don't even notice color; they are just like us." It was this recognition of their differences that allowed the group to survive, not pretending to transcend them. The impulse to unify and separate, rend and join, is powerful and constant.

The Crazy Quilt

THIS QUILT IS OFTEN THOUGHT TO BE THE EASIEST TO make. It is certainly the most common. The *Crazy Quilt*'s roots are in the nineteenth century, and it is not considered, by its detractors, the most skillful or beautiful of quilts. Some call it faddish. It was quite popular during the Great Depression (with nothing, no tiny scrap, wasted) and still has its admirers in the Midwest and the American South.

The women in your circle must contribute odds and ends to the project. They must sit in their places around the large wooden frame, piecing their fabric to the base cloth and cotton batting. As I mentioned earlier, some women enjoy the freedom of form afforded by the *Crazy Quilt*, while others prefer the discipline and predictability of an established pattern.

And you can come to understand other things about the quilters simply by paying attention. Sometimes you can tell what is on their minds from what they avoid saying or the way in which they say it. Or their seating arrangement for the evening. You would think that it would always be the same, unchanged, but it is not. I am reminded of some sort of complicated, intricate dance of many partners, facing many different directions.

The only constant I could discern was the way in which the other quilters hesitated briefly until Anna had chosen her chair.

It is wise to bear in mind that these are polite women in the best sense of the word and that Anna is older than my aunt Glady Joe by eight months, making her the eldest of the group. That fact commands respect even if her role as their leader did not. I know these things from my own observations. If I learned nothing else in grad school, I learned to be a fairly careful witness. (Or maybe I was drawn to grad school because I have always liked to watch.)

For example, Marianna Neale loves the lush wildness of an English garden, but she seldom sews garden quilts, preferring instead more abstract, brilliantly colored quilts. Some of these are almost cubist in design, yet with a subtle, discernible pattern that is almost *sensed* by the viewer rather than *seen*.

(What happens to quilts that are not handed down or acquired by museums or thrown across beds? I read somewhere that they are purchased by a well-known fashion designer and worn by women in New York City or Los Angeles or Chicago— probably seen hailing a cab or dining with friends— skirts with bright patches that swing on the hips.)

Some suggested contributions for the *Crazy Quilt* are: Sophia Richards's child's design in lambs or bunnies; Em Reed's *Double-Wedding Ring* in miniature; Constance Saunders's modified design that is

Chickie's Garden in colors of yellow, peach, salmon, and pale orange; perhaps a location like Glady Joe Cleary's Shenandoah Valley or a famous person or a mythical creature like a mermaid, which interests Hy Dodd; and Anna's fine eye and considerable skill holding it all together.

I'll tell you what makes me happy about marrying Sam, that is, about marrying in general: I know our marriage has just as good a chance of being wonderful as it does of missing the mark. There is a strong possibility that it will be both. And, contrary to what current belief is, it has always been so. This is a tremendous relief. I came to understand this from talking with Anna about the various quilters. However, I am banking on our love for each other to weigh a bit heavier on the "wonderful" side. I do not expect to be wrong about this. It is a matter of faith.

Anna finally made good on her promise to have a long talk with me, quite by accident, I think. She needed to go to San Francisco, and since Sam is living there, I thought we might go together. As I do not have a car, my grandmother and Aunt Glady Joe offered the Chevy wagon, which is heavy and built like a boat, though (I have to admit) quite comfortable inside. It's a good traveling car, they said, and something else about "feeling safe."

So, maybe it was the duration of the trip or my blood relation to Glady Joe and Hy or the nostalgia of the car (I could not help but notice the way in which Anna gently ran her hand over the upholstery, as if the contact between seat and fingertips could unlock some almost forgotten memory); or maybe she had grown accustomed to my presence this summer.

We began by talking about quilting. I learned quite a bit.

Then suddenly she turned to me, the windows rolled down and the wind rushing about the interior of the car, and asked, "What is it you want to know?"

And, to a question like that, what other answer is there besides, "Everything"?

But to return to the *Crazy Quilt*, which has so divided the women.

Which has so joined the women.

As for material, any old, worn, or used clothing would be fine. Corrina Amurri contributes olive drab, over and over, like a problem she is trying to solve. A husband's old shirt is good, or possibly a line of dress buttons, affixed to a patch to look like a string of pearls. Maybe the pearls were given to you as a St. Valentine's Day gift when you were estranged from your man or maybe it is the song that stays with you. Or perhaps you are the gardener of the most elegant garden in all the surrounding counties or you like Kandinsky or Bach or Mondrian or maybe a boy from Chicago fell in love with you on a cattle ranch one summer so many years ago that it all seems like a dream to you now.

Remember, you do not need to tell anyone what your contributions mean and it is more than likely they will hold meaning for you alone anyway. Do not explain. This is your right.

The enchanting new novel by
Whitney Otto

Now
You See
Her

Kiki Shaw is about to turn forty. She doesn't mind
that, except that she's also *disappearing*. Parts of her
that were always there are vanishing, and no one
seems to notice. . . .

"Graceful . . . Poetic . . . Otto's voice is sympathetic
and direct, her imagination equally practical and
romantic."
—*The Philadelphia Inquirer*

Please turn the page to read the first chapter of
NOW YOU SEE HER. . . .

Now You See Her

IN THE WEEKS PRECEDING HER FORTIETH BIRTHDAY, Kiki Shaw made the uncomfortable discovery that she was disappearing. That is one fact of her life.

Another is that she spends her days as a fact researcher for a popular TV game show filmed in Los Angeles. It is her job to invent categories and answers; three categories daily with six answers awaiting six questions, though only five will actually be used.

A third fact of her life, as she reviews her life, is that it seems to consist primarily of Other Lives; that is to say when she recalls her childhood, for example, she remembers the people who lived on her street:

Richard Carter was a pathologist married to Clarisse Carter, a woman chronically "broken down." The Carter children could not have friends over to the house because Mrs. Carter was "resting." Or, if she appeared from the sanctuary of her bedroom, she often had a distant look in her eyes. Possibly chemically induced or the result of too much drink.

Dr. Czarcek was foreign born and his very pretty

wife was also foreign born. Their four children were unruly to the point that most of the neighborhood kids avoided them.

LuAnn Soames drove a blue Dodge and gave out candy to the children.

Mr. Huntington never landscaped his yard and the rumor spread that he was a bachelor who spent his time chasing women and that was the reason for his untended garden and closed shutters.

Mr. Parker did not prefer women at all despite the fact of his marriage and two children. His wife, a husky-voiced European woman, traveled each summer to France, where, it was said, she conducted a string of affairs.

The Newmans had money, owned race horses and gave terrific parties that everyone gladly attended.

Al and Jean Bennett were originally from Indiana. Al worked at one of the studios in the Valley and Jean stayed home, happy, with her brood.

Julie Abbott lived alone and taught school in "town," as Los Angeles was called by these residents of Pasadena. Her parents gave her the money to buy the house, which was as lovingly cared for as Mr. Huntington's was neglected.

The Dorys, an elderly couple, inhabited the smallest house on the street and frequently vacationed in places with names difficult to pronounce.

And the Shaws, Kiki's parents, seemed a classic case of opposites attracting.

Similarly, Kiki can note the people who currently make up her life; a natural listmaker, she takes a break at work, beginning with herself, writes:

What I have:

1. Gainful employment.
2. Three close friends: Nora, Collier and Henry.
3. Two living parents.
4. A small house.
5. Good health.
6. Education.

This last item certainly has not stood up well in the ensuing years. Her education seems to have slipped a bit here and there, although Kiki's job gives her the illusion of recalling something she once knew, as well as attaching a scholarly aspect to her research of some new fact or patch of trivia.

What I want:

Here she decides not to include things like world peace or an end to hunger because Kiki figures that things like cures, peace or satiation are givens. As wishes go.

1. Love.
2. More money.
3. More beauty.
4. Travel.

Since Kiki is bored at work and curious about the desires of other people she knows, she calls up her friend Collier, asks for her list of wants:

1. Love.
2. And, as a subset of Love, to quit the man she is seeing because he is not good for her.

3. More money.
4. More beauty.
5. A new apartment.
6. A new career.

Kiki calls Nora:

> 1. Love.
> 2. A dependable car.
> 3. More money.
> 4. Travel.
> 5. Adventure.

Kiki calls her mother, Gen, now a widow:

1. A man.
   ("Could I say 'love'?" Kiki asked her mother, who only answered, "Call it whatever you want.")
2. Everything.

Kiki, who slides the lists beneath the paperwork on her desk as her boss passes by her door, only pulling them back out when he has gone, cross-references and finds that all want more or less the same things: money, looks, travel—but the top of each list is love. Kiki relates this discovery to Nora, who says, "Are we awful? I mean, is it some sort of weakness that desires love more than satisfying personal ambition or educating yourself or taking off down the road alone?"

"No," says Kiki, "nothing is more important than love. Nothing."

* * *

As with her childhood memories that are essentially about the neighbors on her block, Kiki is incapable of making a list of her own possessions and desires without including those of the people in her life. Instead of lists she could have just as easily typed this:

Collier Grey at forty is a woman who catches the eye, despite her wish for "looks," which appeared on her list. She makes a good living from her own independent video production company, despite her wish for more money. And she sees a man named Gordon who is not good for her.

Nora Barrie was one of those girls in college who were well liked and always seemed to be everywhere at once. She was the one who looked as though she enjoyed wherever she was: a party, a class, the dining hall, the library. She seemed to know everyone—"A speaking acquaintance," she would say—yet somehow remained basically unknown. It could be said she used her warm manner as a wall.

Henry plays cards with Kiki. They have known each other for years and occasionally experience long periods of silence.

Gen is a woman who was certain her life would turn out differently.

Gordon is a man who cannot be true and

Les is the woman he frequently betrays.